wondergirls™

Perfect Harmony

Jillian Brooks

SCHOLASTIC INC.
New York Toronto London Auckland Sydney
Mexico City New Delhi Hong Kong Buenos Aires

ISBN 0-439-35493-5

Copyright © 2002 17th Street Productions,
an Alloy, Inc. company
All rights reserved.
Published by Scholastic Inc.

 Produced by 17th Street Productions,
an Alloy, Inc. company
151 West 26th Street
New York, NY 10001

12 11 10 9 8 7 6 5 4 3 2   2 3 4 5 6 7/0

Printed in the U.S.A.   40
First Scholastic printing, December 2002

chapter
ONE

Letter to all orchestra members

Dear Orchestra Members,

The bus to Chicago for the semifinals will be at the front entrance to the school at 8:30 a.m. SHARP on Friday morning. Please do not be late. Please do not forget to pack your music and instruments, including extra equipment (strings, reeds, etc.) and your performance outfit (white shirt, black pants or skirt). Congratulations on your win at the regional orchestra competition! You worked hard, and you deserve it.

See you Friday,
Ms. McClintic

"Traci! Over here!" I glanced around the lunchroom to see Felicia Fiol, one of my best friends, sitting over by the window. I carried my tray over to the table and sat down. Felicia squinted over at my lunch tray. It was kind of hard to tell what the entrée was supposed to be. Hot chicken salad, they called it.

"I'm so excited about the orchestra trip," said Felicia, nibbling on a carrot stick from the lunch she'd brought from home. She was talking about our trip to Chicago for the semifinal state orchestra competition. Our orchestra had won the regional competition held for schools in our county, and now we would be competing against schools from half of Illinois. "I can't believe we leave tomorrow."

In Chicago, we would get to stay in a hotel right downtown and do some sight-seeing around the city. I had never been to Chicago before, and I absolutely could not wait to see it.

"I'm excited, too," I told her. "It'll be such a blast. But I'm a little nervous about that Mozart piece—you know, the final piece of the program?"

She nodded. "You'll get it, Trace, don't worry."

Felicia plays first flute in the orchestra. She's really good—a natural musician. I don't think you could say that about me. I play in the orchestra mostly because my mom is the orchestra director, and she'd be really disappointed if I didn't.

"There's a sign-up sheet for seating on the bus," she said. "I signed us up to sit together. And there's also a sign-up sheet for rooming partners. What did your mom say about us rooming together?"

"Well, when I brought it up with her, she just

launched into how she couldn't wait to share a room with me and how lucky it was for us because we won't have to pay extra money for another room."

"So should I try to find someone else?" Felicia asked. She looked kind of bummed.

"No, not yet. Maybe I'll bring it up in front of my dad. He might help change her mind."

"Okay, good. Hey, here comes Arielle. Arielle!"

Arielle Davis is another one of my best friends. We have our differences sometimes, but I know she's really a good person. She was wearing this amazing turquoise skirt and a black cashmere turtleneck with platform-heeled black boots. She has the best clothes, and her parents even let her wear high heels—something my parents would *never* do. They say it will stunt my growth.

"Hey, you guys!" Arielle called. "You know Bill Reynolds, that new eighth grader who's totally cute? He just smiled and said hi to me in the hall!"

She sat down and took her lunch out of her bag. It was vegetable sushi in a plastic container that held each piece in place. Arielle's the only person I know who eats sushi, but she says it's really good. She carefully took out soy sauce and wasabi and started eating.

"So are you guys so excited about the trip? I can't believe you get to miss school Friday and Monday. You are *so* lucky," she said.

"I'm psyched, but I'm pretty nervous about the music," I told her.

"Oh, come on, you're really good, Traci," she said. "You sounded great at that regional competition."

I smiled. "Yeah, but we're playing this new piece, and it's a lot harder. I'm just afraid I'll mess up. Do you know what it sounds like when a clarinet player makes a mistake? It's about the loudest squeak you ever heard. It's not something you can cover up."

"Traci, you know you can do it," Felicia said. "You just have to keep practicing if you're nervous."

I knew Felicia meant well, but she could already play the piece perfectly. Besides, if you mess up on the flute, no one really notices because the flute is so quiet. She couldn't really understand what it was like to play the clarinet and have to be worried about losing the whole competition because of your mistakes.

"Well, if I end up rooming with my mother, I won't have any choice. She's making me play the piece for her constantly at home. I'm sure that's what she has in mind for Chicago, too."

"What do you mean?" Arielle asked, frowning. "Aren't you and Felicia going to share a room?"

"Well, my mother thinks it would be *fun* to room with me." I made a face. "Plus it'll cost extra if I stay in another room."

"Oh, what a drag," Arielle said sympathetically.

I could tell my mother was a little nervous about

the competition, too. She always talked about how the important thing was to have fun, but I could tell she really wanted to win. It was her first year at the school, and I think she felt like she could really prove herself as a teacher with a big win like this. I hated the thought of letting her down. I would just have to keep practicing.

Just then Amanda sat down. She had bought her lunch, too.

"Jeez, what is this supposed to be?" she said, looking at her tray. "Isn't a salad supposed to be cold? Like a *salad*?"

I laughed. "Yeah, I thought so. I think our cafeteria just likes to be creative."

Amanda shook her head. "Creativity is great. I'm just not sure I like it in my lunch."

Amanda Kepner is the sweetest one of our group. Me and Felicia and Arielle and Amanda spend all our time together, but Amanda is the one I'm closest to. Since I just moved here, I felt pretty lucky to have found such good friends so quickly.

In the first couple of months of school, though, Arielle and I had some pretty big fights. In fact, all four of us had been getting into arguments lately. Sometimes it felt like we were fighting about something almost all the time. After our last big blowup, when we all decided to become friends again, I kind of resolved to turn over a new leaf: no more fighting with my friends. If there was a problem, I'd just talk it out and I'd try to get everyone else to do the same.

After a few more minutes, I heard the unmistakable laugh of Ryan Bradley. Ryan is the class clown, and sometimes he's a little loud. He's pretty funny, though, and as much as I don't like to admit it to myself, he's actually pretty cute, too. He's a good friend, but I tend to get a little nervous when he's around.

"Hey, girls. Mmmm, that hot lunch looks deeelicious! You think they got the shipment of food to the school mixed up with the shipment to Felicia's dad's shelter? Because it looks more like dog food than people food to me."

He was talking about the animal shelter that Felicia's dad runs. Mr. Fiol's got all kinds of animals, and the four of us volunteer there every week. We even started a program at the local hospital called Healing Paws, where we take animals from the shelter to play with sick kids at the hospital. The animals seem to enjoy it, and it really brings a smile to the faces of the kids who participate.

"Ha-ha, Ryan," Amanda said. She was actually eating her "chicken." "What's in your lunch? Bean sprouts and raw cabbage?"

Ryan's mom is a vegetarian, and she packs him some unusual lunches sometimes.

"Nope," he said, opening his lunch bag, "looks like tofu salad and organic chips. Yum!"

"Hey, speaking of the shelter, I wanted to tell you guys something about Healing Paws this weekend," I said to Arielle and Amanda.

"What's up, Trace?" Amanda asked.

"Well, you might not remember, but there's a girl named Jenny who I spent a lot of time with last week."

"I remember her," Arielle said. "She had a hat on because she lost her hair after cancer therapy. So sad."

"Exactly," I said. "But she's *such* a sweet kid, and she has an amazing attitude. Anyway, she spent the whole time playing with that little kitten we named Peanut. The tiny brown one."

"Oh, he's the cutest one," Felicia said, nodding. "He looks like a little fuzz ball."

Ryan rolled his eyes. "Girls and kittens, man." He shook his head and picked a piece of tofu out of his salad. "If it's small and furry, chicks dig it. If I hunkered down and wore a fur coat, you'd be all over *me*."

Arielle snorted and shook her head. "Not likely, Ryan."

"How's Lola?" Amanda asked him. Lola is this *adorable* Saint Bernard puppy that Ryan adopted from the animal shelter.

Ryan's eyes lit up. "She's great. She's starting to get big now, but she's still pretty drooly."

"Gross!" Arielle wrinkled her nose.

"Anyway," I said, "*as I was saying*, I promised Jenny that I would make sure she could play with Peanut again this weekend. Since I won't be there, could you two make sure that happens?"

"Of course," Amanda said.

I knew I could count on Amanda to help out. Arielle had finished her sushi and gone back to examining her nails as I was talking. I wasn't so sure she'd remember.

Arielle is okay, but she tends to get really focused on things that aren't that important to me, like clothes and boys. But we do play soccer together—the same position, even. And we've gotten closer from being on the same team.

"Are you going to make it to soccer practice on Monday afternoon, Traci?" Arielle asked.

"No, we're getting back too late. My mom told all the coaches. She said Coach Talbot was worried because we have that big game the following Saturday," I said, frowning. "I would hate to let the team down."

"Well, why don't you and I get together on Tuesday at lunch or something, and I can go over the drills you missed," Arielle said.

"Really? That would be great, Arielle," I said. She can be really thoughtful sometimes, right when you least expect it.

"So, Traci, Felicia, feeling ready for the big competition?" Ryan grinned, turning back to me. "Are we going to kick some middle school orchestra butt all over the concert hall?"

Ryan is a violin player. He's really talented, and he has a big solo in the upcoming competition. He's good enough not to be nervous at all.

"Traci's nervous," Felicia told him. "Tell her how good she is."

"You? Nervous?" He gave me a goofy surprised look. "I can't believe it. Why would the daughter of the orchestra director be nervous? Don't worry, Traci, the clarinet's such a soft, quiet instrument, no one will ever notice if you make a mistake," he joked.

And I guess that's why I like Ryan. He always seems to understand just what the trouble is and he can make you laugh about it.

Ryan went to sit down at his usual table, and we finished up our lunch and hung out a while in the lunchroom. Pretty soon the bell rang, and we all got up to go to class. On the way out the lunchroom door, we spotted my mother walking in for the next lunch period.

"Hey, Mom!"

"Hi, Ms. McClintic," Arielle and Amanda said.

"Ms. McClintic, can you look at my concert outfit this afternoon and see if it's okay?" Felicia asked her.

"Sure, Felicia, just bring it by homeroom. I'm sure it's fine."

"Oh, Ms. McClintic, my right index finger is broken, I think," Ryan said, holding it up at an angle. "I don't think there's any way I can play in the competition!"

"Very funny, Ryan," my mom said, trying to look stern but laughing, anyway. "Traci, I was looking for you. Let's meet at three-fifteen at the front door, and I'll give you a ride home."

"Okay," I told her.

I used to get a little embarrassed about talking to my mother in front of my friends, but after a while I got used to it. My mom is really pretty cool, as moms go.

Amanda and Felicia and I split off and headed for our earth science class. We were studying global warming, and it was such an interesting topic that I was actually looking forward to getting back to class to learn more.

"Can you believe this stuff we're learning about pollution?" I asked Amanda. "I mean, we're really going to have to start taking care of the environment if we're going to have a healthy planet."

"Yeah." She sighed. "You know, I was talking to my uncle about it, and he was saying global warming hasn't even been proven to exist, but I told him all about what I'd learned in class, and he said he would have to try to find out more about it."

"So you changed his mind?" I asked.

"Well, I at least got him to start thinking about it," she said. "That's a start." We walked into the classroom and took our seats. Unfortunately, we have assigned seating, so Felicia and Amanda sit near each other, but I'm way over on the other side of the room.

Soon our science teacher, Ms. Carrington, came in and started passing out a sheet of paper to each of us.

"What's this?" Amanda asked.

"Pop quiz!" Ms. Carrington said cheerfully. "Just to keep you on your toes."

"Noooo!" Everyone in the class started whining. "It's not fair! You didn't tell us!"

"That's why they call it a pop quiz, you goofballs!" Ms. Carrington said, laughing.

Amanda laughed, too. She was an excellent student and was sure to get an A on the quiz. I figured I'd probably do okay, too. I'd been paying attention in class lately because I really liked the subject.

But it *definitely* made me happy to be missing school on Friday and Monday!

chapter
TWO

Traci's list of things to pack for Chicago

*Three outfits (red sweater and jeans for bus, blue
    shirt and cords for Saturday, turtleneck and
    plaid miniskirt for Sunday)*
Performance clothes (don't forget black shoes)
*Homework (math and science books, literature
    notebook)*
Walkman/CDs
Instrument and music folder
Extra reeds
Toiletries (ask Mom to buy travel-size shampoo)

At the end of school I met Felicia and Arielle at my
locker, and we walked out together. I was finally
learning my way around the school. My old school
back in South Carolina was much smaller, and it was
very easy to get around. Wonder Lake Middle
School, on the other hand, has several different wings
and a confusing maze of hallways. It was great to
finally begin feeling like I belonged there.

"Are you so excited?" Arielle asked. "Have you decided what you're going to bring?"

"I don't know yet," I admitted. "I want to pack light but have enough outfits so I'm not wearing the same thing every day."

"Just bring things you can mix and match," Arielle said. "Bring the jeans you have on . . . and let's see. . . ." Arielle started concentrating. I knew she would give me good advice. When it comes to clothes, she's a pro.

"Okay," she said finally, "I've got it. You should bring your brown cords, that cute little plaid skirt you got at the Gap, and two sweaters. All of those things you can wear together."

"Wow," I said. "You're really good at this. That sounds perfect."

"Plus you and Felicia are about the same size. So you can borrow clothes from each other. You just doubled your wardrobe right there."

"Awesome." I laughed.

Amanda met us near the door, and we all hugged one another good-bye. It was pouring rain outside as Amanda, Felicia, and Arielle dashed out the door and ran for the bus stop.

I went to the front steps to wait for my mom. As usual, she was kind of late. Just as I was starting to get bored, Ryan stopped by to say hello. When I saw him approaching, I could feel myself starting to smile. I tried to hide it, though.

"Hey, McClintic," he said. "Holding up the wall?"

I was leaning against the front of the building. I rolled my eyes. "Hey, Ryan, what's up?"

"Just going home to practice a little before I have to go to church tonight."

"Yeah, I think I'm going to do a lot of practicing tonight, too."

"Don't worry, Traci," Ryan said, smiling. "I know you're going to knock 'em dead."

"Thanks, Ryan. I appreciate it."

He took off down the steps in the rain toward the bike rack. For some reason, Ryan's encouragement really made me feel great. At that moment, I was sure I *would* be great in the concert. All I needed to do was practice.

Just then my mom came out the front door. She was juggling a bunch of loose papers and carrying her big leather briefcase, purse, and gym bag. She saw me, smiled, and dropped her purse and gym bag on the steps.

"Let me get those, Mom."

"Thanks, hon. Oh, boy, have I got a lot to do tonight."

My mom can be a little disorganized at times, but she's really a great mother. I should know; I spend a lot of time with her. Not only is she the orchestra director, she's my homeroom teacher, too. About the only time I don't see my mother is when I'm out on the soccer field.

I loaded our stuff into our minivan and then got my bike and loaded that into the back. Sometimes I ride my bike to and from school, but since it was pouring rain, I was happy to have a ride in the car.

"So, Trace," Mom began as soon as we pulled out of the school driveway, "I was thinking . . ."

I knew this was going to be about practicing the clarinet.

". . . maybe we could do a little practice session before dinner."

I tried to hide my frown. "Sure, Mom, no problem. I need the practice."

"Okay, then if we have time, we could squeeze one in after dinner, too."

My heart sank, but I knew I couldn't say no. My mom was just as nervous as I was about the concert—maybe more. "Okay," I said, trying to look cheerful.

Suddenly, a figure came into view on the side of the road.

"Traci, is that Ryan Bradley on that bike? We should offer him a lift."

I squinted through the windshield. I couldn't tell from so far away. But as we got closer, I could see that sure enough, it was Ryan, getting completely soaked, pedaling through the downpour with his violin case sticking out from the top of his backpack. My mom pulled over.

"Ryan, can we give you a ride?" I shouted to him

15

through the window. "We'll just put your bike in the back."

Ryan grinned. Water droplets dripped from the ends of his hair and down his face. "What if I just hang on to the bumper and water-ski?"

Mom laughed. She opened the back of the minivan, and he stowed his bike and jumped in the backseat.

"Thanks, Ms. McC. You practically saved my life out there. I'm not the best swimmer."

"Actually, I was more concerned about your violin," my mom said. "Or do you have the waterproof kind?"

I couldn't help but wince. I was embarrassed by my mother's lame joke, but at least she tries.

"Nope, but I think the case shuts tight enough to keep it dry," Ryan said with a grin. "I hope."

"So are you excited about the trip, Ryan?" my mother asked him.

"Right. I've been meaning to talk to you about that. I think you should consider incorporating a Stupid Maniacs song into the concert program."

"What's he talking about, Traci?" she whispered to me, laughing. "What in the world is Stupid Maniacs?"

I was trying not to giggle. "It's a rap group, Mom," I told her. "They sing that song 'Power to the People.'" I was just glad she knew he was joking.

She laughed. "Oh, okay, Ryan. That's a great idea. How about if as an assignment you listen to the song and transcribe it and write the music for each instrument in the orchestra?"

"Sure, no problem," he said in a mock-serious voice. "I'll have that ready for you tomorrow."

A few minutes later we got to his house, and he jumped out of the car, then got his bike out. His mother came to the door and waved at us as we pulled out. We waved back, and I called good-bye to Ryan.

"What a great kid that Ryan is," my mother said as we drove home.

As soon as we got home, we started practicing, my mom at the piano in the living room and me standing next to her with my music on a stand. Every time I made a mistake—and there were too many times—I could see her wincing. She never got mad. Still, I felt lousy.

My brother, Dave, got home while we were practicing. He and I normally argue a lot, but when he saw us practicing for the zillionth time, he gave me a sympathetic look.

He goes to Wonder Lake Middle School, too, but he's in eighth grade and naturally thinks he's the coolest. He used to play trumpet back when he was in sixth grade, but he was so bad, my mother finally let him quit. I think she got tired of constantly nagging him to practice.

I guess that's why I felt kind of obligated to be good at the clarinet. I think my mom would be pretty bummed if at least one of her kids didn't play an instrument. After all, she *is* a music teacher.

Anyway, even though Dave looked sympathetic, I felt a flash of anger at him for quitting the trumpet. Maybe it would have been him standing in the living room with my mom instead of me. But then I remembered how earsplittingly bad he really was, and I abandoned that fantasy.

My mom took a five-second break to greet him.

"Hi, sweetheart. How was school?"

"Hi, Mom. Hi, dork," he said. "School was fine. I'm going over to Jacob's."

"All right," my mom said, "but come home for dinner. We're having chicken."

"Okay, Mom. Have fun, Trace," he said, grinning.

My mom and I carried on for another half hour, and then I went upstairs to start my homework. I could hear my mom getting dinner ready downstairs, and then my dad came home. He's a pediatrician, and he really loves what he does. Actually, we moved here so he could start a clinic for kids with no health insurance. I'm really proud of my dad. He's a great doctor, and he uses that skill to help people. I want to be like that when I grow up.

I ran downstairs to greet him.

"Hi, Dad!"

"Hi, honey! How was your day?"

"Great," I told him as we walked into the kitchen together.

"Ah, roast chicken! My favorite! Hello, sweetheart, I missed you today," he said, kissing my mother.

"Oh, Bob, I missed you, too. How was work?"

I set the table while they talked. As my mom was putting dinner on the table, Dave came through the back door. "Hey, Dad. Roast chicken, awesome!"

We all sat down and dug in.

"Pretty soon we're going to be on our own, Davy, when the gals go to Chicago," my dad said with a wink.

"Yeah, Dad, we can eat pizza every night!"

"We'll eat in front of the TV."

"Good idea. We'll eat pizza and chips and watch the football play-offs every night."

"And then *Babewatch*."

I couldn't help laughing at the idea of my dad and Dave sitting in front of the TV, eating pizza, burping, and swearing like a couple of bachelors.

"So are you two looking forward to the trip to Chicago?"

"Oh yeah. I think it's going to be a great experience," my mother replied.

"What about you, Traci? Are you nervous about the competition?"

"No, Bob!" My mother answered for me, giving a funny little laugh. "Don't be silly! Why should she be nervous? She's going to play wonderfully. And it's not about the competition, anyway. It's about having *fun!*"

"Hmmm, okay," said my dad. The look on his face told me that he wasn't so sure about my mom's answer. "Do you feel the same way, Traci?"

I glanced at my mom for a second, then took a deep breath. "Well, I guess I'm a little nervous, Dad," I admitted. "I *have* been kind of messing up on the new piece we're doing—"

"You just need more practice, Traci," my mom jumped in. "We'll practice again after dinner and as much as we can before we leave."

"Now, don't overdo it, Hillary," my dad said to my mom. "Don't forget about the main objective of doing orchestra, like you just said. It's about having fun."

I looked from my dad to my mom. If only he were going with us to Chicago! This seemed like a perfect time to bring up the subject of the rooming situation at the hotel in Chicago. My dad was already pulling for me about the clarinet practice. There was a good chance he would see my side of the story about sharing a room with Felicia instead of my mother.

"Hey, Mom, I was thinking," I began. "Felicia was asking me if I would share a room with her in Chicago, and I wondered if maybe it might be better for you not to have me in your hair while you're preparing for the competition."

My mom frowned. "What do you mean, honey? You could never be in my hair. I think it will be so much fun to share a room with you. I mean, how often do we get to stay in a hotel together? Plus we can use that time to practice."

I tried to hide my disappointment. "Yeah, I guess so," I mumbled.

"Wait a minute, Hillary," my dad interjected. "Maybe Traci would have more fun if she got to share with a friend." *My hero!*

My mom seemed to consider that. "Well, the thing is," she said after a moment, "it will cost an extra seventy-five dollars if she stays in another room. It'll be free if we stay together. Don't forget, Bob, that I'm having to finance a big part of this trip. Remember, you reminded me the other day that we need to stick to our monthly household budget."

My dad paused for a minute and looked up at the ceiling, like he was thinking. "Well, what if Traci agreed to pay for part of the expense out of her allowance?"

"I could do that!" I said quickly, trying not to sound too excited. I didn't want to hurt my mom's feelings.

"I guess that might work," Mom said slowly. She looked like she was thinking. "And you're probably right about it being more fun for her to stay with a friend. I didn't really think of that. I guess I've been pretty preoccupied with the whole competition part."

"Are you sure it would be okay, Mom?" I asked. "Because staying with you would be all right, too."

21

"Of course it's okay, Traci. And if you wanted to stay with Felicia, you should have told me sooner. I don't mind, sweetie. I should've thought of it myself."

"Great. Thanks, Mom."

After dinner I ran upstairs to call Felicia and tell her the good news. But when I got her on the phone and told her, I could tell by her voice that something was wrong.

"What's up, Felicia?" I asked her. "You sound kind of funny."

"No, I'm fine. I'm sorry. I really am excited that we're rooming together. It's just that Penny's been here all afternoon, and now she's staying for dinner, too."

Penny is Amanda's baby-sitter, and now she's Felicia's dad's girlfriend, too. Penny's really nice, but it kind of bothers Felicia to see her dad with a woman who isn't her mother. Mr. and Mrs. Fiol divorced not that long ago, and Felicia lives with her mother on weekends and with her father during the week.

"I'm sorry, Felicia. Are you okay?"

"Yeah, I guess so. I mean, Penny is fine and everything, but whenever she's here, I just get in a bad mood. I can't seem to help it."

"Well, then, let's talk about something that will take your mind off it."

"Okay," Felicia said. "Like what?"

"Let's see. . . . Tell me what clothes you're packing for Chicago."

"Oh, good idea! I was going to wear those brown corduroys with the embroidered pockets and my green sweater for the first day. And I thought my black jeans for the second day. Do you think my red cardigan looks good with those?"

"Yeah, totally. And if you bring it, then I can wear it with my plaid skirt on the last day."

"Okay." She laughed. "Good plan."

We talked for a while about clothes and the trip.

"So did you already do the math homework?" Felicia asked after a few minutes.

"Yeah, it was kind of hard. You want me to give you the answers?" I joked. Felicia is a good student, and she would never copy anybody else's homework.

"No thanks! Oh, man, I'd better get going on it. I want to try to finish it before dinner so I can practice flute before bed. I think it sticks in my brain better if I practice right before going to sleep."

"Hmmm . . . maybe I'll try that," I said.

As I hung up the phone, I heard my mother calling from downstairs. I sighed and grabbed my clarinet, resigning myself to a final practice session before leaving for Chicago.

chapter
THREE

Sign hung above the rearview mirror on the charter bus:

<u>BUS RULES</u>
No eating
No beverages
Stay in your seats at all times
unless using rest room
No gum chewing
No radios
No shouting or loud talking
No ball throwing
No cursing
Aisles must be kept clear
at all times

The next day dawned bright and sunny. I woke up so excited that I jumped out of bed and ran right downstairs. My dad was eating breakfast and reading the paper.

"Look who's up early," he said. "Are you too excited to sleep?"

"Yeah!" I told him. "I can't believe we actually leave today."

"Well, believe it." My dad winked at me. "Good luck at the competition, Trace. And whatever you do, don't forget to have fun."

"Thanks, Dad." I gave him a hug as my mom came downstairs. We all had breakfast, and then my mom and I headed to school.

Everyone was waiting by the bus when we arrived. We were a little late because my mother couldn't find her notes for the concert. We spent about half an hour looking for them, and then she found them right in her briefcase. Everyone thought that was pretty funny.

It took a while to fit the instruments and everybody's luggage in the baggage compartment. We had to wait in line to hand the driver our things. He had just finished wrestling a tuba into the remaining space when I handed him my clarinet case.

"Here's a sensible girl, with a reasonable-size instrument! You're very smart not to play the drums or the French horn."

I couldn't help but giggle as Felicia handed him her flute case.

"Oh, and this is a breath of fresh air! A tiny little flute. You're my favorite girl from Wonder Lake High!"

"Middle school!" Felicia said, laughing. "We're

25

Wonder Lake Middle School. I'm only in the sixth grade!"

"Only in the sixth grade? You look much, much older."

Then my mom walked up.

"You're in high school, though, right?" he asked her.

My mother threw back her head and laughed. "Yes, I was in high school about seventy-five years ago, before there were automobiles like this bus here."

"I remember," he said. "I think we were in the same class."

They had a good laugh at this, but all the kids just looked at each other. *Grown-up humor*. We shrugged.

We all boarded the bus, and Felicia and I sat down near the back. I got the window seat, but we agreed to switch in the middle so we'd both have it for half the time.

We checked out how the seats reclined and tried out the reading lights and air conditioners. Finally, we were on our way!

My mom led us in a round of songs, and at first everyone sang loudly and laughed hysterically, but by the second hour of the trip, when we had gotten to fifty-five bottles of beer on the wall, the singing sort of died down.

The bus driver's list of rules turned out to be much stricter than he was. And Ryan seemed like he was

out to break every rule before we got anywhere nea..
Chicago. He got up and came and perched on the
arm of the aisle seat and told us some stories about
the hotel. He had once stayed there with his parents
and said it had a pool, a gym, a sauna, and really great
views of downtown Chicago, if you got a room on a
high enough floor.

I hoped we would—that sounded so incredible.
Actually, I had never even stayed in a hotel before. I
had stayed at motels on vacations, and on the drive
from Charleston to Wonder Lake, but never in a
real fancy hotel. I was so excited, I could hardly
stand it, but I tried to hide my excitement. I didn't
want to look like some kind of backwoods hick to
Ryan. I mean, he already made fun of my southern
accent all the time—he even liked to call me "Dixie
Chick."

The truth is, the four-hour drive really flew by.
Before I knew it, we were in sight of the Chicago sky-
line. Felicia and I had switched seats, but it didn't
matter because I was sitting almost on her lap, trying
to get a look out the window.

"Wow! Is that the Sears Tower?" I asked Felicia.

"Yeah, and look at the building next to it!"

The city looked huge, so full of people and exciting things to do. It was nothing like boring, familiar
Wonder Lake. I looked at the tall buildings and tried
to imagine being grown-up and having my own

apartment way up in the sky. I decided right there and then that I would live in a big city someday.

When we pulled up in front of the hotel, which was a huge twenty-five-story building, my mom got up to check us in.

"Everybody please stay in your seats while I go inside. That means you, Ryan, if you even remember where your seat is!"

I giggled. Ryan had been wandering around making conversation with everybody for almost the whole trip. He looked around the bus and scrunched up his eyebrows, then finally headed to his original seat near the back.

After about ten minutes, my mom came back with a sheet of paper and a stack of what looked like credit cards.

"Okay, I have everyone's room assignments here. The girls will be on the nineteenth floor and the boys will be on the twenty-first floor. As I call your name, please come up and get your key cards. Then go and wait on the curb for your luggage."

"Key cards?" I asked Felicia.

"They're like credit cards, with a magnetic stripe on the back to open the lock on your room."

"That is *so* cool."

Finally, my mom called us. I picked up our key cards, and we went out to the sidewalk and waited in the chilly air. The driver passed out our bags and instruments, and we all headed toward the doors. A doorman in a fancy red suit and hat smiled at us and held the doors open. "Welcome to Chicago," he said with a wink. We all walked into the huge wood-paneled lobby and gawked as we found our way to the elevators.

"Look at this place!" Felicia said wonderingly. "There's a fountain right in the lobby! This is amazing!"

I had to admit, she was right. The hotel felt more like a mansion than the motels we'd stayed at along the highway. There was a group of hotel clerks standing behind the check-in desks, and they smiled and waved as we walked by. "Good luck at your competition!" a tall man with a beard called.

"Wow," I muttered, plopping my bag on the floor near the elevators. "We're definitely not in Wonder Lake anymore."

As we stood waiting for the elevators to come, my mom spoke up loudly so we would all hear her.

"*Musicians!* Please go up to your rooms and settle in and make sure you're in the ballroom with your instruments by one-thirty for practice."

My heart sank at the thought of practice. I had made the same mistakes when I practiced with my mom after dinner last night that I had been making all along. I dreaded messing up in front of the whole orchestra, especially with everyone so psyched to win the competition.

But nothing could really dim my excitement when we opened up the door to our room and saw the incredible view from our window. We were so high up, it made me dizzy to look down at the ground.

We ran all around the room, checking everything out.

"Felicia! Look at this," I called from the bathroom. "They gave us soap, shampoo, and conditioner with the hotel's name on them."

"Cool! And the toilet has a ribbon around it." She and I cracked up at the SANITIZED strip around the toilet seat that showed it had been cleaned.

We bounced on the beds, jumping from one to the other until we were sweaty and exhausted.

Then we decided to call Ryan. We got his number from the front desk.

"Wait!" Felicia said as I started to dial. "I have an idea. Pretend you're a girl from another school who saw him in the lobby and thought he was cute."

"But he won't believe it. How would she know his number?"

"Say you asked another kid from our school what his name was," she suggested.

"Okay," I said, giggling, then dialed the number while Felicia got on the other phone across the room.

Ryan's roommate, Charles, answered, and I tried to disguise my voice when I asked for Ryan. It was all I could do not to burst out laughing. I knew I couldn't look at Felicia or I would lose it.

"Hello?" Ryan said.

"Hi," I said in my disguised voice. "Is this Ryan?"

"Yeah, who is this?"

"Well, my name's Ashley. I go to . . . James Joyce Middle School. We're in the competition, too, and I . . . um . . . saw you in the lobby. I just wanted to say hi." I was almost dying from holding back my laughter.

"Really?" he said. "Well, that sure is nice of you. How did you know my number?"

"I asked one of the kids from your group what your name was. Then I called the front desk."

I accidentally let out a snorting laugh, then tried to cover it up with a cough.

"Are you all right there, Ashley? You sound a little stuffy."

"Yeah, sorry, just a bad cold."

"Well, Ashley, I think I might have noticed you in the lobby, too."

"Really? Um . . . did you see me looking at you?"

"Yeah, maybe," Ryan said. "Were you the girl in the blue dress with the blond hair, about a hundred years old, with the mustache and the stinky armpits? Because I saw you, and I really thought you were cute. What do you say we get together for dinner later out in the back alley by the Dumpster?"

Felicia and I nearly fell out of our chairs with laughter. Darn! We should have known that Ryan Bradley, king of the pranksters, would recognize a good prank when he heard it. When we recovered a little, he told us to meet him at his room and he'd show us around the hotel. Eager to see the rest of this palace, we grabbed our key cards and headed up.

"Hi, Ashley," he said, answering the door. "Did you do something to your hair? You look much younger."

We took the elevator to the basement, where we saw the pool and the gym. Felicia and I went into the women's locker room and checked out the sauna. We couldn't figure out what was supposed to be so great about a sauna, which felt like the hottest room in the world. I guess sweating is supposed to be good for you or something.

Then we went to the lobby and saw the dining room. Kids from other schools in the competition were wandering all around. Ryan showed us the ballroom where we would be having practice; the hotel staff was already setting up chairs.

We decided to go to the business center on the second floor to see if we had any e-mail. We figured Amanda and Arielle might have written us, and they would want a report about how we were doing.

There was a short line to wait for a computer, and as we stood there talking, I noticed a boy who kept looking over at me and trying to catch my eye. I looked at him, and he smiled like maybe he knew me. I smiled back but then looked away. *What a weirdo*, I thought. He was still looking my way.

Finally our turn came on the computer. I logged on, and we all checked our e-mail from my account.

Amanda and Arielle had sent a message together to both of us from the school computer room.

```
Hi T and F,
   You are so lucky you get to miss math AND com-
puter science. Mr. Firth is making us do a paper
on the history of the personal computer because
he said so many people did so badly on the quiz.
Five pages by Monday. Like we don't have enough
to do this weekend! We will miss you tomorrow at
Healing Paws (we'll remember about Jenny and
Peanut, Trace, don't worry!). Don't practice too
hard, and don't come home without that trophy!
                    Love,
                    A and A
P.S. Say hi to Ryan.
```

We wrote them back.

```
Hey you guys,
   We're in the business center at the hotel.
You should see the view from our rooms: AMAZ-
ING! Sorry we missed out on doing that paper,
but I'm sure Mr. Firth will make us do it next
week. We have our first practice this after-
noon. Wish us luck. More later, time for lunch!
                    Tons o' love,
                    T, F, and R
```

"I'm starving!" Felicia said.

"Yeah. Me too," Ryan said. "And we can get a look at the competition in there while we eat. I think everybody eats together."

A dining room was set up so that all the kids in the semifinals could eat together in one big room. There were two buffet tables set up at one end of the room, and long tables that seated about twenty each were set up in a semicircle. You could see all the other tables from wherever you were sitting.

As people walked in at one end of the room, they grabbed a tray and a plate and served themselves, then chose a table wherever and sat down.

Kids were here from all over the state, all in middle school, and you could sort of tell which groups were together by the way they were dressed.

One group all had on really preppy, nice clothes, and another had big baggy pants and sweatshirts.

I wondered how we must look to everybody else. Pretty middle-of-the-road, I guessed. We all had neat, normal clothes on and kind of regular haircuts.

It got me thinking, though, about what was *normal* and what wasn't. The kids with baggy clothes probably thought they looked completely normal and we were the strange ones! It was good to get to see people from other places, I decided. It gave you a bigger picture of the world.

We could see where the rest of our group had sat

down at the far end of the room and waved to them. Some friends of Ryan's from the string section had saved us seats, which they pointed to.

"What a view from our rooms, huh?" said a clarinet player named Bill as we sat down and started eating.

"I know. It's fantastic," Felicia said.

A girl named Wendy said, "The only thing is that the boys got to be on a higher floor than we did. That doesn't seem quite *fair.*" She was joking, but you can't joke around Ryan without getting a joke back.

"I know. Boys are taller in the first place!" he said with a goofy look.

"Oh, Ryan, you know what I mean." Wendy giggled. Was it just me, or did all girls pay extra attention to Ryan?

"I don't think it makes that much of a difference, anyway," said Ryan. "You guys can see all the way to Canada, too, right?"

Wendy laughed and laughed, even though the joke was *not* that funny.

As I was glancing around the dining room, I caught sight of the kid who had been looking at me in the business center. He was eating lunch with his friends. I got a good look at him this time because he couldn't see me.

He's actually pretty cute, I thought. But then I looked over at Ryan. . . .

He was much cuter.

chapter
FOUR

CHICAGO SCHEDULE

(Please try to be on time—if you are late, you keep fifty people waiting!)

FRIDAY
11:00 Arrive at hotel
12:30 Lunch
1:30–4:00 Full practice in ballroom
6:00 Dinner

SATURDAY
7:30 Breakfast
8:30–10:00 Practice with your section
12:00 Lunch
2:30 Meet in lobby for Sears Tower trip
6:00 Dinner

SUNDAY
7:30 Breakfast
10:00–12:00 Final practice!

12:30 Lunch
2:00 Performance!
5:30 Awards presentation
6:00 Dinner

MONDAY

7:30 Breakfast
8:30 Meet in lobby with bags and instruments
9:30–12:00 Museum of Contemporary Art
12:00 Return to Wonder Lake

After lunch we ran up to our rooms to get our instruments for practice. On the way back down, the elevator made a stop on the sixteenth floor. A bunch of boys got on with their instruments, and I noticed that the guy who had been staring at me was one of them. He didn't see me at first, and I saw that he was carrying a clarinet case, too. He ended up standing right next to me, and I couldn't avoid looking at him. He smiled at me and looked at his case and mine and said, "Hi."

He had seemed kind of strange earlier, but now he seemed nice enough. Plus he was a fellow clarinet player. I said hey back. He looked like he was going to say something more to me, but by the time he took a breath to speak, the elevator doors opened onto the lobby and we all got off and scattered in different directions to our practice locations. I wasn't really in the mood to talk, anyway. I was starting to get that familiar nervous feeling in my stomach, thinking about the practice.

We walked over to one of the smaller ballrooms, which was Wonder Lake's designated practice location.

"Hi, sweetheart. Hi, Felicia!" my mom said as we arrived. "Can you two start setting up while I finish arranging the chairs?"

"Sure, Mom," I told her.

Felicia and I followed my mother around and set up the music stands in front of the chairs she was arranging. We put a stand in front of every third chair for people on either side to share.

We knew exactly how the setup looked because we had to do this all the time in the gym, where we practiced back in Wonder Lake.

I pictured our gym back home, probably filled with basketball players having practice right now. I wondered what everybody else was doing, having their regular day while we were here in a totally new place. I felt really lucky. But then a little piece of me wished I were with them—so I wouldn't have to be playing the clarinet.

"Girls, I'll get the rest of this. You two had better get tuned up," my mom said.

I could feel my nervousness building as the rest of the orchestra came straggling in. Everyone started to take out their instruments and put them together, and soon there was the din of fifty people softly practicing different snippets of song and making adjustments to the sound of their instruments.

Felicia and I finished up with the stands, and I went over to put my clarinet together. I put a reed in my mouth to soften it and looked around at all the other reed instrument players—oboes, saxophones, clarinets. They all had reeds sticking out of their mouths, too.

A reed—a small oblong piece of springy cane—goes in the mouthpiece of a reed instrument, and it's the vibration of the reed that makes the instrument's sound. But a reed has to be primed to play properly. It has to be moist and soft, and so a reed-instrument player warms up a reed by putting it in his or her mouth.

"Have you been practicing that hard section in the Mozart piece?" my friend Jen asked me as she adjusted the fingering on her instrument. She plays first clarinet. I play seventh—second to last.

I took the reed out of my mouth. "Are you kidding? I've been practicing with my mom nonstop. I'm still a little shaky on it, though."

"Don't worry, you'll do fine," Jen told me. Easy for her to say—she's really excellent.

I felt pretty good as practice started. We did some simple pieces first, just to warm up.

"Okay, musicians, you're sounding great. Let's play our opening piece and pretend it's the competition!"

On my first try, I got through it without a hitch, and my confidence really started to go up. We played all the songs in the program but the last song, and I didn't make any mistakes at all. But what I was really nervous about was the last piece. I was playing so well, though, that it seemed a little less daunting than usual.

Then I saw something that made my stomach do a flip-flop.

Kids from another school had gathered in the doorway of the ballroom. Their own practice must have ended earlier than ours, and they were listening to us practice! Suddenly, I was petrified.

"Well, Wonder Lake, you are really sounding terrific," my mom said. "And I see we have an audience over there, so play your very best and let's scare the pants off them for the competition! Let's play our final piece and see how it sounds."

My hands shook as we started to play. I could feel all of the other kids' eyes on me. I got through the first part of the piece okay, but that part was easy. As the hard part approached, I tried to take deep breaths to calm down. Then it began. The rest of the music quieted, and the clarinets dominated the music in a series of complicated quick scales. I began okay, but suddenly my clarinet let out a bunch of loud squeaks and chirps instead of the music. My mother stopped us by tapping her baton on her music stand.

"That's okay, that's okay, clarinets. Let's just start it again from four bars back. Trumpets, you should be even quieter. I should hardly hear you. This section is about the clarinets. And two and three and . . ."

We began again, with my hands shaking and my face bright red from embarrassment. I almost knew it was going to happen again . . . and of course it did. TAP, TAP, TAP, my mother stopped the music again.

"No problem, clarinets, let's just try it again." My mother was trying to smile, but I could see that it was forced. I could not believe I was messing up in front of the competition and disappointing my mother at the same time. I was mortified. I decided I wouldn't play another note. I would just pretend.

I moved my fingers and tried to look like I was blowing into my instrument on the third run-through. I glanced up at my mother to see if she could tell.

She was looking at me with a frown.

It's pretty hard to put one over on her when it comes to music. I knew she'd be mad, but at least the rest of the orchestra wouldn't try to throw me out of the twenty-first-floor window for ruining their chances at winning the competition.

We wrapped up and I went over to my clarinet case, not looking anybody in the eye. I had to concentrate on just trying not to cry. Everybody was really nice, but I still felt terrible.

"Don't worry, Trace," Ryan said. "It kind of sounds like experimental music the way you play it. We'll get extra points for creativity."

I tried to laugh but couldn't really manage anything more than a weak smile.

Felicia came over with a sympathetic look on her face. "That's what practice is for, Traci, to work these problems out."

"But all those other kids heard me mess up!" I felt like crying again.

"That doesn't matter. What matters is the competition," she told me, putting a hand on my shoulder. I was glad when she left to pack up her flute. It was nice that she was trying, but I just couldn't have felt worse.

At least I didn't think I could have felt any worse. But then I saw the cute clarinet player from the elevator. He was walking over to me, and I realized that he had heard my terrible playing. And now I was going to have to talk to him. I prayed to disappear into the floor.

But it didn't happen.

"Hey. I'm Adam. I'm from Collindale."

"Hi, I'm Traci," I muttered. "Nice to meet you."

I forced myself to stand up straight and look him in the eye. Adam had light blond hair, even lighter than mine, that was cut short and sort of spiky. He had light blue eyes, about the color of a robin's egg. I had to admit, looking at him this close up, he was very cute. Just not my type, I guess.

"You know, you might not feel like it now, but I think you're a really good clarinet player."

I tried to stifle a laugh. "Yeah, right. I mean, thanks for being polite, but I'm sure you just heard me," I said.

"No, really. I've always had trouble with exactly the same things in pieces like that. I think the problem is that when you get nervous, your breathing pattern gets interrupted, and so you don't blow properly."

"Well, no offense, but that's kind of obvious. I know the problem is my technique," I said. Was he making fun of me? I mean, *duh*, of course I wasn't blowing properly. It wasn't like I thought those squawks were part of the music or something.

Adam smiled. "But there are breathing techniques you can do to solve the problem. I know because I really had to work on it myself. It isn't that you're a bad player—it's just a question of breathing."

I paused and looked him in the eye. "Do you really think so?" I was starting to believe him. In fact, I really *wanted* to believe him. It sure felt great to hear someone show that kind of confidence in me.

"Sure I do. I could show you what I mean if you want. I could teach you a technique to even out your breathing."

"Really? Do you think it would help? Do you think I could learn it that quickly?"

"Oh, for sure. There's nothing to it. Why don't we get together tomorrow morning for a little while if you want? I need my clarinet to show you what I mean."

"Wow. That is so nice of you. That would be great, if you really don't mind."

"No, I don't mind at all. Why don't we meet in our practice room early tomorrow morning? It's meeting room C. We don't start practicing until eleven."

"Okay, I'll be there."

"And don't forget to bring your clarinet. Is nine o'clock okay?"

"Yeah, that works for me," I said, and I couldn't help but smile. I'd have to miss most of our section practice, but if Adam could really help me, I knew it would be worth it.

Just then Felicia and Ryan came back over, looking at Adam curiously.

"You guys, this is Adam. He plays in the orchestra from Collindale. He's a clarinet player, too. Adam, this is Ryan . . . and this is Felicia."

"Hey, Adam," Felicia said, "nice to meet you."

"Hi, howzitgoin'?" Ryan said.

"Hi," was Adam's only reply.

"Adam is going to teach me some breathing techniques to help me with my little squeaking problem," I said, laughing.

Adam laughed, too. "Okay, so I'll see you in the morning, Traci. It was so nice to meet you." He started to walk away.

"You too, Adam. Bye!"

"Uh, bye," Felicia said, but Adam was too far away

to hear her and didn't say good-bye to either of them.

"Hmmm," Felicia said, looking peeved.

"You certainly cheered up fast," Ryan said in a kind of annoyed voice.

"Well, I feel like he could really help me," I told him. "Plus he was really sweet. He told me he thought I was a good musician."

"He didn't seem that nice to me," Ryan said. "Think about it, Traci, we're here for a competition. Why would he help you play better? It just means he stands less of a chance to win."

It was rare to see Ryan be serious like this. Usually he was really easygoing and almost nothing bothered him. But right now he seemed really upset.

"I don't know, Ryan, maybe he cares more about music than just competing for some trophy," I said.

Ryan snorted.

Now Felicia looked a little mad, too. "You know, Traci, I care about music, too, but that's not just 'some trophy.' We worked hard to get here, and I'm really proud of that."

"I know, Felicia," I said. "I'm sorry. I just think he was a nice guy who wants to help out a fellow clarinet player."

"Yeah, maybe," Ryan said, scowling. "Or maybe he's actually a special clarinet angel from heaven, sent down from the woodwind gods to help you."

Felicia laughed at this, but I just kept putting my

instrument away without saying anything. So what if they didn't like Adam? He was really nice to me, and it seemed like maybe he knew what he was talking about. Maybe he really could help me.

"I have to go talk to my mom, y'all. I'll see you up in our room, Felicia?"

"Okay, see you."

As the two of them walked out of the ballroom, I went over to my mother. She was talking to one of the drummers about something, and she held up one finger to me and smiled, asking me to wait a minute.

I was nervous about talking to her. How terrible would it feel to be the director of the orchestra and have your own daughter be the very worst player? *Well*, I thought, *maybe Adam can help me fix this problem of mine, and I'll be able to make my mother proud.*

Finally, she came over.

"Traci, I know you must be worried about that last piece, but it's not okay to only pretend to play your instrument."

"But Mom, I just really didn't want to make a big mistake again. And with all those kids watching." Again I felt like I was going to start crying.

"I know, Traci, but it's dishonest, and unless you play the piece, you're never going to be able to perform it under pressure."

"Yeah, I'm really sorry."

"Honey, I'm about twenty minutes late for the meeting of all the orchestra directors. We're going to get together and discuss the rules of the competition."

"Okay, so do you have to go?"

"Yes, but I'll stop by your room in about an hour, and we can talk."

"Okay, thanks, Mom," I said, and started to turn and walk away.

"Oh, and Traci?"

"Yeah, Mom?"

"Don't worry, hon, you're going to do great."

I hope so. I smiled. "Thanks, Mom. See you upstairs."

She was being nice about it, but I knew she was probably just as worried as I was. I just hoped Adam's help would be the miracle I needed to get through this thing.

chapter
FIVE

Felicia was watching TV when I walked into the
room. She gave me a big grin and said, "Hey, watch
this!"

She jumped up on the bed and bounced a few
times, then did a pretty good flip from one bed to the
other.

"Nice one! Let me try."

Pretty soon we were laughing hysterically. I
couldn't really get the hang of the flip and kept ending up wedged in the space between the mattress and
the wall. This made Felicia laugh harder.

"You know I'm trying to give myself a concussion so I don't have to play in the competition?"

"Great idea!" she said. "Maybe if you break both your legs, you won't have to take next week's science exam, either."

This got me laughing even harder. We jumped until we were exhausted and I had completely forgotten my troubles.

Then came a knock at the door.

"Oh, that's my mom, I guess," I told Felicia. "I have a feeling she's going to want me to practice with her."

Felicia opened the door.

"Hi, Ms. McClintic!"

"Hi, Felicia," my mom said. "Hey, would you mind giving us a couple of minutes to talk alone?"

"Sure, no problem," Felicia said, throwing me a sympathetic look. "I'll go up to Ryan's and see what he's doing. See you at dinner, Trace. Bye, Ms. McClintic."

Felicia shut the door behind her, and my feeling of disappointment and dread came rushing back to me.

Mom and I sat down opposite each other on the beds Felicia and I had just been trampolining on.

"What happened in here? It looks like a hurricane hit," said my mother, looking around at the mess we'd made. "Well, anyway, honey. I want you to know that I know you've been working very, very hard, and I'm proud of that."

"Thanks, Mom. But I know it's a disappointment."

"The only way I would be disappointed is if I knew you weren't trying," she said.

"But Mom, what if we lose the competition because of me? Why can't I just not play that part of the last song? I'll move my fingers, and the judges will never know."

"Traci, I can't believe you're even suggesting that. You know that's like lying. And that part is written for eight clarinets. You'll compromise the music itself if you don't play it."

"It just seems like it would be so much easier," I said, looking down at the floor.

"Listen, Traci, we are going to practice and just get through this thing. I think your problem is just in your breathing. And I think it happens only when you get nervous. We can work on that," she said.

"Hey, that's exactly what Adam said!" I told her, brightening.

"Who's Adam?" my mom asked.

"He's a clarinet player from the Collindale team. They were the ones listening to us at practice. He heard me and said the exact same thing about breathing that you did. Plus he offered to work with me to teach me a breathing technique that can even out my breath when I'm nervous."

My mom nodded. "That's great, honey. It might work. It seems pretty nice of him to offer to help you when he's on an opposing team," she said.

"I think he's just a really nice guy," I said.

"Well, Traci, what do you say we just run through the last piece a few times before dinner? We have about twenty minutes."

I groaned inwardly, but I knew that it could only help me.

I took out my clarinet again, and I warmed up a little with easy stuff. I could feel myself getting tense and nervous.

"I know all this practicing is a pain, Traci. But I think if you knew the music a little better, the piece would flow for you and you wouldn't get so nervous," my mother said.

That seemed to make sense. "Maybe you're right, Mom."

But when we got to the difficult scales in the Mozart piece, all that I could play was terrible noise.

I saw my mother wincing as if she were being pinched, but she struggled to keep on smiling.

I felt like crying again. It didn't seem like this was helping me in the least.

I could only hope that Adam's help tomorrow would magically fix everything.

After what felt like a lifetime of practicing, it was finally time for dinner. My mom and I put away my clarinet and took the elevator downstairs.

When we got to the dining room, my mom and I got plates of food at the buffet, and I looked around for Ryan and Felicia. They didn't seem to be there yet.

"Oh, Traci, there's Tom and Midge. I'm going to go sit with them. Will you be okay until Felicia and Ryan get here?"

I looked around the ballroom again and nodded. I really didn't want to sit with the other chaperons, so hopefully Ryan and Felicia would get here soon.

"Come to my room at seven-thirty," my mom continued, "and we'll go over that music one more time."

"Sure, Mom. I'll see you then."

Tom and Midge Worth were the parents of an eighth-grade trumpet player named Tom Worth, Jr. They were nice but kind of boring. Mr. Worth was an accountant, and he always wanted to talk about what we were studying in math. I like to be friendly, but I just don't enjoy whole conversations about long division. I really didn't want to sit with them, but after standing there with my plate for a few minutes, Felicia and Ryan still hadn't shown up.

Just then I saw Adam. He was waving at me from across the room and calling me over, pointing to an empty chair next to him. He had saved me a seat! I was really surprised. I walked over and sat down. "Hey, Adam. Thanks. I was about to have to sit with my mo—I mean, the chaperons."

I decided that Adam didn't need to know that I was the orchestra director's daughter. It's not that I'm embarrassed by my mother—I mean, not exactly. I just figured I didn't really need to start explaining right then.

"Traci, meet the rest of the orchestra. This is Matt, Kristin, Paul . . ." and he went down the row, saying each of their names.

"Hi, Traci," they all said. I could see by the way everyone paid attention that Adam must be kind of the leader of the group.

"And over there is the sixth-grade table. We don't let them eat with us. This table is for upperclassmen only," Adam told me.

Should I tell him I was a sixth grader? Or just let it go? I felt funny letting him think I was older—that was almost like lying. So I decided to try to say it in a funny way.

"Well, I'm a sixth grader—should I just go over there and eat with them?"

Adam laughed. "No, I knew you were in sixth grade. But you seem pretty mature."

I couldn't help smiling. He thought I seemed mature? "How did you know I was in sixth grade?" I asked him.

"I looked your name up in the concert directory."

"Hey, look at that guy!" one of Adam's friends said. "He looks like he's going to a seventies costume party! Check out that shirt!"

They all laughed and looked at the kid he was pointing at, a smallish redhead who noticed that they

...king about him and immediately hung his head.

"What a loser!" someone else said.

I frowned. They were being so mean! It was obvious that the kid they were making fun of could hear them.

Adam wasn't really laughing, though. He was more just paying attention to me. Maybe he didn't think this kind of joke was funny.

I really hoped not.

He asked me questions about myself—what I liked to do besides play in the orchestra and what my school was like—and seemed to be really listening to the answers. I told him about my friends and about Healing Paws, and we got into a nice conversation. In the background, though, his friends kept making fun of people who were walking through the dining room and also swearing like crazy! Really nasty words that I wouldn't even use if I stubbed my toe.

Then I saw Ryan and Felicia coming over.

"Hey, Traci. Hi, Adam. How's it going?" Felicia said. She was smiling, and it looked like she was willing to give Adam a second chance. Ryan didn't look too happy, though.

"Hey, you guys!" I said. "This is some more of the Collindale team." I tried to introduce some of them, but I had forgotten their names, and most of them didn't even bother to look up. I looked to Adam for help, but he looked at me like I was making a fool of myself. Just by trying to introduce my friends!

"Hey, we're gonna kick your butts on Sunday!" someone said from the other end of the table.

"Yeah," someone else said. "We heard you play . . . and you're totally lame."

They all laughed. Even Adam. I guessed this was just the way they joked.

But Felicia and Ryan looked at each other and frowned. "We'll see you later, Traci," Ryan muttered as they turned away.

I thought about getting up and going after them, but I really didn't want to look like a dork. "Bye, you guys," I said quietly.

Just then Adam turned back to me and smiled and asked me how long I'd been playing the clarinet. When he told me he thought I was excellent, I forgot I was bummed at all and told myself that he was actually really nice. As dinner went on, we kept on talking. I started to feel really comfortable again.

While we ate our dessert, apple pie, I looked over at Felicia and Ryan at the Wonder Lake table. I didn't want them to feel like I had blown them off. I was a little worried, but I thought, *I'll just make sure I hang out with them after dinner.*

But when I finished eating and brought my tray up, Adam said, "We're going to play Ping-Pong in the game room. Do you want to play? You and I can be a doubles team."

"Okay, that sounds like fun," I said. The truth was, I really was enjoying myself with Adam. And since he was going out of his way to help me, I thought it was only right to be friendly and get to know him.

"But let me warn you," Adam said, "I'm not that great at Ping-Pong. I need someone good on my team so I don't get clobbered." We both laughed.

I tried not to look over at Ryan and Felicia as I left. I was having fun, and I didn't want to feel guilty about it just because they couldn't get along with Adam and his friends.

We went to the game room and had a blast. I guess Adam was lying about being no good at the game. We beat everyone! We played until it was time to go and meet my mom to practice.

I felt kind of bad about not hanging out with Felicia. But I hoped she would understand. I had just met Adam, and it was kind of fun to hang out with seventh graders. Adam was really nice—at least, when no one else was around. And it made me feel great to hear someone say I was a good musician.

My mom was making some notes on our concert music when I got to her room.

"Hi, Traci. I just talked to Dad. He said to tell you he misses you."

"How do you think he and Dave are doing without us?" I asked.

"Well, Dad said Dave was making dinner, and

so far he hadn't burned down the house," she said.

"Don't you think it'll be a huge mess when we get back? I don't think they would know how to load the dishwasher if their lives depended on it," I said.

"No, I'm sure it's a mess now, but I bet they'll clean like crazy before we get home, just to show us how self-sufficient they are."

I laughed. "Yeah, you're probably right."

"So I saw you eating dinner with some other team. Were you with the boy you told me about from Collindale?"

"Yeah, I was. And then we all went and played Ping-Pong. They're pretty nice," I told her as I put together my clarinet.

"Well, Collindale has a great orchestra. Apparently they're very well-known, and they usually win these competitions."

"But not this year, right?" I said with a smile.

"That's right!" My mom grinned. "Not this year! This is Wonder Lake's year!"

Wonder Lake Middle School had never even won the regional competition before. If we won here, we'd go on to the state finals. And obviously it was just a fantasy, but from there, the Illinois state winners went on to the national competition in New York City. I knew my mother dreamed of winning.

Meanwhile, my dream was getting through the concert without ruining her chances. I promised myself that I would practice until I knew the music effortlessly so that when I met with Adam in the morning, I could concentrate on learning the breathing technique for this song.

I played the song over and over and then over and over again.

At eight-thirty, my mother said, "Okay, hon, I think we've done enough for tonight. You seem like you know the music pretty well, and I'm just exhausted."

"Come on, Mom, just a couple more times," I said, and kept playing.

My mother lay down on her bed. "Traci, why don't you go down and practice with Felicia? I'm really tired."

I had beaten my mother at her own game. I actually wore *her* out with all the practicing! But there was no way I'd get better if I didn't keep working.

I packed up and went down to our room, psyched to hang out with Felicia and tell her about Adam. But when I got to our room, she was asleep in front of the TV. I tried to wake her up, whispering, "Felicia! Felicia!" But she just groaned and rolled over, away from the light.

I really wanted to talk to her, but there was no way she was going to wake up.

I lay down on the bed and suddenly felt so tired, I could barely move. This had been a really long day. I forced myself to get up to wash my face and change into pajamas before I fell asleep.

I watched the TV for a minute. A Shauna Ferris video was on—she's my favorite singer. I wondered if she'd ever felt moments of doubt like I was feeling.

Did she ever lie awake at night, worrying about a concert the next day?

Somehow I really doubted it.

chapter
six

Techniques for relaxing while performing:
1. Take slow, even breaths
2. Ignore audience—concentrate on music
3. Picture waves at the beach
4. Aaargh! Quit clarinet and take up the triangle!

"Traci, wake up," I heard Felicia say. I lifted my head groggily and looked at the clock. It was already eight-thirty, and I was supposed to meet Adam at nine.

Felicia was running around the room, getting dressed and doing her hair. We'd missed breakfast, and we were supposed to be at a section practice session right then!

"How did we sleep so late?" I said, jumping up and making my way to the shower.

"I don't even remember falling asleep," she said. "What time did you come in?"

"Around nine."

"Oh, really? Did you have fun with the cool Collindale crowd?" she asked, not looking at me.

"Well, I played Ping-Pong with them for a little bit, but I was practicing with my mother for most of the night."

"Hmph," she said, still not looking at me. I could tell something was bothering her, but I sure didn't have time to ask her what was wrong right then. I had to get ready and go to practice. I made a note to myself to talk to her later about what was wrong.

A section practice is when you get together with the other players of your instrument and work on your music. No one took these sessions too seriously, so it wasn't a big deal to be late.

But I wasn't going at all.

I had been planning on going at eight-thirty and then leaving to meet Adam at nine, but now I was just going to have to go straight to Adam's.

"I'll see you at lunch!" I called to Felicia as she went dashing out to go and meet the flutes.

I got out of the shower and spent a minute figuring out what to wear. I wanted to look good, but I didn't want to look like I was trying to look good. I put on my plaid skirt and Felicia's green sweater, but I checked myself out in the mirror and thought I looked like I was trying too hard. Finally, I settled on my jeans and Felicia's sweater.

I put my wet hair back in a ponytail—there was no time to dry it—and gathered up my music.

I was afraid of running into my mother on the elevator. She was planning to stop by each section practice to check in, so there was a chance I would see her on her way somewhere.

She'd find out I wasn't in the practice when she saw the rest of the clarinet players, and I just hoped that what I learned from Adam would make it worth how mad she was going to get.

I met Adam in the Collindale practice room on the second floor. The Collindale kids were allowed to practice there at any time, but since it was so early, we were the only people there. Adam smiled when I walked in. "Hi, Traci. Wow, that green looks good on you."

"Thanks," I said. I was kind of flattered but also starting to suspect that his motivation for helping me was not purely in the name of the betterment of music. He was definitely looking at me like he thought of me as more than just a friend and a fellow clarinet player. I wasn't sure how to react, so I decided to ignore it.

"Let me just get my clarinet ready, and we can get started," I said.

Once I got the instrument together, I set up my music on a stand, and we sat down across from each other on two chairs.

"So play something just to warm up," Adam told me.

I played some sections of easier pieces of music that I knew by heart, and Adam sat nodding. I was a little nervous, but I was playing all right.

"So now play it and think about your breathing. See how you don't have to pay attention to it, but that it's just natural and even? That's the goal for the harder pieces, too."

"But the problem is that I get nervous, and I can't control my breathing."

"Exactly. See, you already know about the problem, and that's the first step toward solving it," he said.

He was making sense. Maybe this would really work. I hoped so.

"Okay," he said, "now play something that you don't feel that confident about."

I started to get nervous as I got out the music for the Mozart piece.

"Are you getting nervous about this piece before you even start playing it?" he asked.

I frowned. "Well, I guess I am."

"Yeah, I can tell just by looking at you. So now concentrate on what happens when you get nervous. If you figure out what the effects are, hopefully you can start to control them."

"Okay, well, I can feel my heart speed up, and my hands are shaking a little." I held them up for him to see. "And like you said, my breathing is changing."

"How is it changing?" he asked.

"Let's see. . . . It's faster, and I'm not breathing as deep," I said.

"Exactly. Now let's hear you play the piece," he said.

"But now it's even worse because we were talking about it," I said. There was no way I'd be able to play it now!

"That's okay. You have to see how you play when you're nervous in order to fix the problem. Just give it a try."

I played the piece. I almost immediately started squeaking away, getting more nervous and embarrassed, which made it even worse. About halfway through, I just stopped.

"I really can't do this anymore," I said to him. I was sweating.

"That's okay, I think we can work with that," Adam said, laughing, which made me laugh, too.

"Yeah, that's about as bad as it gets, I'd say," I agreed.

"So now you'll try to control your breathing. Whenever you feel your body start to show signs of nervousness, this is what you do," he said.

He showed me how to breathe in and out on a count of four, making sure I took a breath deep into my lungs and not just a shallow breath like you do when you're nervous.

"Okay, the next step is to match your breathing to the music when you're really nervous. So depending on how fast you're breathing, count one-two-three-four or one-two-three to the beat of the song. This way you're doing it without having to think about it. It's just part of the music."

I tried it on an easy piece and felt like I was starting to get the hang of it.

"That's great. Now all you have to remember is to take a deep breath and fill your lungs each time."

"How did you learn all this?"

"I have a great teacher who was a professional musician. This is one of the first things he taught me. He said that controlling your nervousness is just as important as knowing the music really well or knowing how to place your fingers on the instrument. A musician has to learn to perform under pressure. It's just a part of learning."

"Wow," was all I could say.

After a while I felt like I had gotten the hang of it completely, and Adam declared that it was time for me to try the new technique on the difficult piece.

Again I got nervous as I was preparing to play it. But I just took my deep breaths and tried to stay aware of what my body was doing.

I matched my breathing to the tempo of the song and began. . . .

Suddenly, I found myself playing it perfectly. All the notes that I was normally terrified of just floated out of my clarinet like a birdsong.

I finished in amazement. I was elated.

"Wow. That was incredible, Traci. I never expected you to pick up the technique that quickly," Adam said.

"I'd better try it again. Maybe that was a fluke," I said.

I took a moment, thought about my breathing like Adam had shown me, and began again.

Again I played it perfectly, without a hitch.

I was so happy, I could have danced around!

"So that's it, Traci. Looks like you got it."

"Thank you *so* much, Adam. You can't imagine how much I appreciate it. This is the greatest thing I've ever learned."

"It's really no problem," he said, smiling.

"So I haven't heard your team play. What's in the program for you at the competition?" I asked him, concentrating on my task.

"Honestly, the music we're playing is so much more advanced than what you guys are doing, I'd be surprised if you'd even heard of the pieces," he said.

It seemed like kind of a rude thing to say, but I was too happy about my new breathing technique to get offended.

"Yes, I heard that Collindale usually wins the semi-finals and has even been to nationals a few times. You must have a good director."

"Yeah, we do, and that makes all the difference, really. I mean, no offense, but your orchestra director seems like she has all she can handle just getting her shoes tied. I can't imagine her having the ability to teach advanced music."

I froze, and my throat constricted. Of course Adam didn't know she was my mother. But I didn't say anything. I just gave a lame laugh.

I felt terrible not defending my own mother, but I really didn't know what to do. Adam had just done me this huge favor. Maybe he didn't intend for it to sound as mean as it did—maybe he was just trying to be funny. If that was the case, I didn't want to make him feel really bad by acting all offended.

Still, I felt really weird.

"Traci?"

I looked up. That wasn't Adam's voice—it sounded like Ryan! Sure enough, when I looked over, Ryan was standing in the doorway. I stood up. *Oh no!* Had my mom noticed I'd skipped the rehearsal and sent Ryan to come to get me?

Ryan didn't seem upset, though. He looked around the room casually. "So, um, what are you guys doing here?"

"We're *rehearsing*." Adam stood up from his chair and frowned at Ryan. It seemed like he really didn't want Ryan there. "And you're interrupting."

"Oh, am I?" Ryan tried to look all innocent for Adam. "Oh, excuse me for bothering you, Your Royal Highness." Suddenly, Ryan's expression changed, and he pulled a pack of gum, a rubber ball, and a small apple out of his pocket. "I just thought the king could use some entertainment." With that, he started tossing the objects in the air, and it took me a few seconds to figure out that he was trying to juggle. I couldn't help laughing—Ryan can't juggle at *all*. I could see that he was really trying, but pretty soon all three of the objects were on the floor. The apple hit the hard wood with a mushy *thunk*.

Adam shook his head. He looked really upset. "What are you doing? You weren't invited here, and you're completely interrupting our practice with your lame jokes. How old are you, six?"

I frowned. Ryan *was* being goofy, but it seemed like Adam was being meaner than he deserved. Ryan was down on the floor, picking up his stuff, but I could see his ears turning red with embarrassment.

"Look, I thought you were supposed to rehearse with your *own* orchestra," Ryan said. He looked up at me, then back at Adam. "I just came here to see if Traci knew she was missing our section practice. I thought she might like to come for the last few minutes." Ryan glanced back at me, looking curious.

I didn't know what to do, really. Adam was being a lot of help, but I *did* feel bad abandoning my own team. Still, I had told Ryan that I was rehearsing with Adam this morning and would be missing most of the section practice. So why was he trying to make me stop now? Was it possible that he was *jealous* that I was spending time with Adam? As soon as I thought that, I could feel myself blushing. Quickly, I sat back down and picked up my clarinet.

"I don't think so, Ryan," I said, trying to hide my blush by looking down at my music. "I'm really learning a lot here. I'll catch up with Wonder Lake later."

"Well, okay." Ryan shoved his gum and rubber ball back in his pocket. He sort of sounded like he didn't believe I wasn't coming. "Suit yourself, I guess." He glanced over at Adam. "Later, King Collindale." He walked out of the room.

"Whatever," Adam muttered under his breath. "That guy's so immature. A total jerk. Why do you hang around with him?"

I looked up at him in surprise. I couldn't believe Adam was so upset! Ryan was acting kind of silly, but it seemed like Adam was being the jerk. "Because he's my *friend*." I started packing up my clarinet and music. "Maybe he's right. Maybe I should catch the last few minutes of *our* practice."

"No, wait." Immediately Adam came over and took the music out of my hand. "I'm sorry if I offended you. I guess I was upset because he interrupted our practice, and I feel like we were making a lot of progress. Don't you think?"

Slowly, I nodded. I had to admit that I felt more

confident playing with Adam than I had this whole year of school. "Yeah, I do."

"Then let's keep working, okay?" Adam smiled and walked back over to his chair. "Let's go through the piece one more time."

On the way back to my room a little while later, I tried to make sense of the whole scene with Ryan and Adam. It had brought out some weird behavior in both of them. Ryan seemed to really be bothered by Adam. I couldn't help wondering why he had such strong feelings about him. I mean, Adam was kind of a strong personality, but usually Ryan could get along with everybody.

I wondered if there were a chance that Ryan had the same feelings for me as I seemed to have for him. The way he was acting was just the way a jealous person would act.

As I turned the corner to walk toward the elevators, I caught sight of my mother heading toward the elevators, too, from the other direction.

I gasped and jumped back.

Had she seen me? I didn't think so. I looked around for a place to go in case she came toward me. I knew how mad she was going to be that I'd skipped our practice, and I wasn't ready to face her just yet.

I turned the corner and stood for a minute in front of a big flower arrangement, waiting for my mom to

70

go up in the elevator. I could hear the *pings* of elevators arriving and departing, and soon I figured that she had to be gone. Slowly, I crept around the corner and looked at the elevator bank. The coast was clear. I walked over and pressed the up button, letting out a sigh. Actually, I was beginning to feel a little silly.

It was my own mother, after all. Why was I hiding from her when I was going to have to explain it all to her eventually, anyway?

She was going to be mad, but wait until she heard how well I could play the piece now. By the time I got to the nineteenth floor, I was perfectly calm again. I smiled as the elevator door opened and headed confidently toward my room.

chapter
SEVEN

Message left for Felicia on hotel room voice mail:

"Hi, Felicia, it's Dad! Penny and I just wanted to call and see how it was going and to tell you good luck. Miss you! Call when you get a chance. Bye for now!"

I couldn't wait to tell Felicia what Ryan had done. And I also couldn't wait to play her the final piece in its new and improved form. I was just so excited.

"Hey, Felicia," I said as I walked in. "I'm so psyched you're here!"

She was lying on her stomach with her head propped up on her elbows, chewing on one of her fingernails. A cartoon was playing on the TV.

"Hi, Traci," she said unenthusiastically. I was sure she'd cheer up after she heard my story.

"So listen to this. I was with Adam, and he was showing me—"

"Yeah, I know. Your mother was here looking for you. She's really mad."

"Well, but listen. She won't be mad anymore when

she hears that I can play the piece now. I can play it perfectly, Felicia! Wait until you hear. But first I have to tell you what Ryan did."

But Felicia wasn't even looking at me. She was just staring at the TV.

"Felicia, what's wrong?" I asked. I was dying to tell her what had happened.

"Nothing."

"Come on, seriously, tell me what's going on. You're acting like you're upset about something."

"No, I'm not. I'm just watching TV."

"Felicia. Just tell me."

She looked up at me. "Well, it's just that I've barely seen you since we got here. I thought that since we were rooming together, we'd hang out together, but I've just been alone for most of the time. Now I wish I'd roomed with someone else."

That seemed like kind of a mean thing to say, but I was willing to give Felicia the benefit of the doubt.

"But I've been practicing."

"Were you practicing when you left with Adam last night from dinner?" she asked.

"No, but I was only with him for a little while. Then I went up to my mother's room and practiced for two hours. We came here for a competition. Pretty much the only things I've done without you are things that will help us win."

"If all you were going to do is practice, you should have just roomed with your mother."

I looked at her. On the one hand, she was being a little mean, but on the other hand, she was a little bit right. I did feel bad about just leaving with the Collindale crowd last night. Plus Felicia is really sensitive, and I didn't want to have any problems so close to the competition. I reminded myself what I'd decided before we left—that I would try to keep the peace with my friends, no matter what. No more letting little things blow up into big fights.

I decided to apologize.

"I'm sorry, Felicia. You're right," I said. "I promise I will spend more time with you. It's not really fair that you're ending up hanging out alone. Let's spend the rest of the day together."

She hesitated, looking at me. I think she was surprised that I said I was sorry so quickly.

"Okay. Thanks, Traci," she said, and smiled at me. "Should we start by doing some gymnastics?" and then she jumped up onto the bed and started doing flips.

I got up and joined her, and we worked out a routine where we both jumped at the same time and flipped to opposite beds. Then we put on MTV and made up a jumping and flipping dance to the videos that came on.

We were screaming with laughter and singing along with the videos and just basically being completely wild when I heard a pounding at the door.

I went to answer it and opened the door to my mother's furious face.

Felicia saw her, grabbed the remote, and turned off the TV.

"First of all," she began, "I've been knocking for five minutes! I don't know what you're doing in here, but this is a hotel room, not a gymnasium. You need to be a little more responsible with the freedom we've given you here and treat this space with more respect."

"Sorry, Ms. McClintic. We got a little carried away," Felicia said.

"We will, Mom. I'm sorry, too."

She didn't respond to this but just kept talking. "Second of all, and most important, Traci, is that you had the bad judgment to miss a practice this morning. I'd like to know where you were and why you thought it would be okay to just ignore your responsibilities to your teammates."

"Mom, listen, I know you're really mad, but if you'll just hear me out, you're going to be so happy," I said, walking over to my clarinet case.

"Traci, don't walk away from me. We're talking."

"I have to get out my clarinet, Mom. Trust me. Instead of going to section practice this morning, I went and met with that kid from Collindale I told you about, Adam."

"I don't remember your asking my permission to miss practice, Traci. And you can be sure I wouldn't have given it to you, so this excuse is not helping your case."

I was putting the instrument together as she spoke. "Adam taught me this breathing technique this morning, and I think you might change your mind when you hear me play. Just give me a chance."

"This better be good, Traci," my mother said.

I took a moment to focus. I was really nervous. If I couldn't play as well as I did with Adam, my mom was going to hit the roof. Everything was riding on this moment.

But I took my time and thought about my breathing in time with the music, like Adam had taught me. Then I started to play. I risked it and went straight into the hardest piece without even warming up. I just felt like I could do it.

And I could. I played it perfectly, just like in the morning. My mother looked amazed. And then, just to show her I could, I played it again, and it was just as good. I was amazed myself.

"Traci, I'm still mad that you skipped practice without my permission, but that was terrific, honey. I mean, that was just great."

"Thanks, Mom."

"How did you do it?" she asked.

"Well, I focus on my breathing when I get nervous

76

and take deep breaths to the tempo of the music. I can't believe how easy it is once you get the hang of it."

"Astonishing. You'll have to teach me this technique."

"Sure." We all laughed.

"Yeah, me too." Felicia said. "I wasn't too crazy about that Adam guy, but he seems to know what he's talking about."

"Play it again," my mom said with a big smile. I knew she was happy for me but also relieved for herself. After all, this was her moment in the limelight, too.

I played it again perfectly, and this time my mom and Felicia clapped and cheered loudly.

"Traci, I'm proud of you, but not proud of the way you did it. Next time you need to ask my permission if you want to skip practice."

"But you just said you would have said no," I said with a smile.

"Well, that's true, but it's my job as your mother to get mad when I don't know where you are. And I was worried about you."

"I know. I really am sorry, Mom. I just had a feeling it would be worth it," I said as I started to take apart my clarinet for the millionth time that day.

"Well, I guess it was," she said grudgingly, and we all laughed again. It felt great to laugh. I had been worried for so long. Finally, things were looking up.

My mother looked really happy now, and I was so relieved.

"I have to tell you girls about the meeting with the orchestra directors. We got together to discuss the competition," my mother said.

"Did they all just decide to forfeit before we play because they know they can't beat us?" Felicia asked.

"Yes, they did," my mother said. "But before they go home, they're going to throw their instruments in the lake because we're so good, they don't know how they can ever play again."

We all giggled hysterically.

"Actually, girls, I think we really do have a good chance of winning."

"Really?" I asked.

"Yes. We met with the judges, and they explained that they will judge on level of proficiency, which means how well you play. But they will take into account the difficulty of the music the orchestras are playing."

"Are we playing music that's harder than the other schools'?" Felicia asked.

"Yes, we really are playing advanced material. The only team that is more advanced is Collindale. Their orchestra program is very well developed. Most of the kids start playing when they are very young."

"But we could still beat them, right?" I asked.

"You bet we can!" my mom said, smiling.

"Who are the judges, anyway?" Felicia asked her.

"There are ten of them, and they're musicians and conductors from the Chicago area. For each performance, they each give a point score, and those are averaged to figure out the winner."

"And the awards ceremony is right after the performances, right?"

"Yes. There'll be awards for best section—like woodwind or horn. And each instrument will get a best soloist award. And then they'll announce the best overall at the end," my mother said.

"I really want to come home with that trophy," Felicia said.

"The trophy would be nice, but you know, girls, winning's not the most important thing. The most important thing—"

"Is making beautiful music!" we all finished together. My mom got a kick out of that. We all laughed for a while.

My mother really is the best. Not too many moms are as cool as she is, I thought.

"Should we all head to lunch?" my mom asked.

"Yeah, I'm starving," Felicia said.

We walked down the long hall to the elevator. The hotel was really big, and it was easy to get lost at first. After my time in the stairwell, I was getting a little more familiar with the place. We got on the elevator, which was pretty small, considering what a big hotel this was. It was all mirrors on each wall and the doors, and it was like looking at yourself into infinity.

The elevator stopped at each floor, and kids from the competition got on—all going to lunch.

On the sixteenth floor a new bunch of kids got on, and I realized after a minute or two that Adam was among them. But there were too many people crammed onto the elevator for me to say hello, and he hadn't even seen me yet.

"Oh, I just remembered, I have to go down to the garage to get my dress for tomorrow out of the bus. I put it in the overhead bin and forgot it, and now I'm sure it'll need to be pressed," my mom said as we were stopping at the lobby. "I'm staying on to the garage level. I'll see you girls later."

"Hey, Traci!" Adam said. He had turned around and was holding the elevator door for us to get off.

"Okay, bye, Ms. McClintic," Felicia said as we stepped into the lobby. "Hi, Adam."

My mom raised her eyebrows in recognition of Adam's name, like she expected to be introduced. But instead I just choked and said, "Bye, Ms. McClintic."

My mother's eyes opened wide in shock as the elevator doors closed.

Adam tried to make conversation as we walked to the dining room, but I couldn't listen because I felt so awful. For that moment on the elevator, I just hadn't wanted Adam to know that the flaky Ms. McClintic was my

80

mother. But now I felt totally ashamed of myself.

Felicia kept looking at me as I murmured responses to what Adam was saying, and after we got our food, the Collindale kids went to their own table.

Felicia stopped and turned to me and opened her mouth to say something—obviously to ask me about it. But I just said, "I know. Don't make me feel worse."

Felicia pulled me aside. "Listen, Traci, you may not want to talk about it, but whenever this guy Adam is around, it seems like somebody's feelings get hurt."

"Felicia, I already feel bad enough. I'll just apologize to my mother, and it'll be fine," I said impatiently. I knew I was snapping at her because I felt guilty, but I couldn't help myself.

"It's just that we had such a great conversation with your mom, and she was so nice about you going to meet Adam instead of practice—"

"Felicia," I cut her off. "I know I made a mistake. I don't need you to hit me over the head with it."

"Okay," she said. "Sorry. It was just the look on your mom's face."

"I know. But listen, I just remembered. I have got to tell you what happened while I was practicing with Adam. It was so funny!"

But just then we got interrupted by Wendy, who came up from behind us.

"Missed you in section practice, Traci," she said with a hint of anger.

I was sure the clarinets had spent the practice wondering where I was and worrying that I would be the one to screw up the whole section in the performance.

"I know, Wendy. I was in a special tutoring session. When you hear me play, you'll know what I mean," I told her.

"It's true, Wendy. Traci is flawless now. Wait until you hear," Felicia said, backing me up.

"Okay," she said, sounding doubtful. "If you say so."

chapter
EIGHT

Lunch menu for orchestra competitors

Baked chicken
French fries or baked potato
Peas
Dessert
Beverage of choice

As Felicia and I sat down next to Ryan, I could see that he was pouting a little, probably mad because I didn't leave with him to go to the section practice. I felt bad, but at the same time, I still wasn't really sure why he had bothered to try to come get me. I decided not to mention it at all.

"Hey, Traci," Ryan greeted me casually. "Hey, Felicia. How are you two today?"

"Great, Ryan, how are you?" Felicia asked.

"Oh, just fine, thanks. Traci? Are you well?"

"Yeah, I'm good, Ryan. Thanks for asking." I said, chewing on a piece of chicken.

"How was your practice with the King of Cool from Collindale?"

"Actually, it was great. He taught me a breathing technique that really makes a huge difference. I can play the music perfectly now," I said, smiling.

"Oh yeah? That's great, Trace," he said. Then he poked at his peas. It was kind of gross. I wondered whether he was ever going to eat them.

Then all at once Ryan started loading peas into his straw.

"What are you doing, Ryan?" Felicia said.

"It may become necessary to defend our territory," Ryan said, calmly placing the loaded straw down on the table. He glanced darkly across the dining room.

He was looking at Collindale's table. Adam.

I looked at Felicia, but she just seemed confused by this comment. Then I looked at Ryan, but his expression didn't tell me much. He turned back to his meal, picking at his french fries and the remaining peas. It must be hard to be a vegetarian at these kinds of buffets, I realized. They didn't really seem to offer any vegetarian options.

"So, how did the practice go?" I asked.

"It was okay . . ." Felicia started, but then she dropped off. I looked over at her but saw that she was looking at Ryan. Ryan didn't seem to be paying attention to us anymore. He was staring behind me, watching somebody approach. I turned around. Oh *no*.

Adam.

This time he was with a bunch of his snooty friends.

I started to say hello, but he wasn't even looking at me. He was looking at Ryan.

"There he is," Adam said to his friends. "This here is the loser who thinks he's some kind of court jester. Or maybe a clown."

"Yeah, he looks like a clown," one of his friends said. I could see that Ryan's ears had started turning red again. I looked at Adam, trying to figure out what he was aiming at, but he wasn't looking at me.

"Where's your big red nose, clown?" another one of Adam's friends asked.

"Hey, listen," Ryan said, sitting up. "Cut it out. I'm sorry I interrupted your practice. Let's just drop it."

"I don't want to drop it." Adam glared at him. "You're completely lame. From now on, I want you to leave us alone."

Us? Did he mean him and me? I opened my mouth to protest, but before I could, Ryan turned around to the table. He was reaching for something. All at once I realized what he was doing and pushed away from the table.

Ryan brought the straw to his lips and let the first pea fly, and it missed Adam by inches. Adam saw it, and the expression on his face darkened. He backed away from the table, and Ryan's next shot hit him on the shoulder.

"That's really mature, clown," Adam said as his friends scattered and ran back to their table. "Stop it. That's not funny."

But Ryan had reloaded and took aim again as Adam continued to stand there. Adam tried to duck, but Ryan anticipated it and hit him with one-two-three peas to the face.

"Cut it *out*, dude!" Adam yelled at Ryan.

Ryan just laughed as he reloaded. "Not so brave without your friends, huh? Why don't you try to defend yourself or just go away?"

Felicia was laughing hysterically at this point, but I thought Ryan was going too far.

Adam's face was a mask of rage. "Stop it *now*, you pathetic clown! Or we'll take it outside and my friends will help me kick your lame butt!!" he shouted at Ryan.

The whole table stopped talking and eating and looked over at the two of them. It was silent all around.

Ryan just stared at Adam. Nobody at our school ever talked to anyone like that, and I could tell Ryan was shocked. His ears were bright red. It was hard to embarrass Ryan, but I was pretty sure Adam had done it.

I could tell Ryan was trying to think of something funny to say to cut the tension, but he was just too shocked to come up with anything.

"Take it easy, man," is what he finally said. "It's just a joke."

"Really funny joke," Adam spat, brushing peas off his sweater. "Traci, I'll talk to you later, when you're not hanging around with kindergartners."

Then he turned and walked quickly away.

I turned to Ryan. He was just sitting there, looking kind of sheepish. In a way I felt bad for him, but I was also really mad at him for embarrassing me in front of Adam. "Ryan, that was too much. Haven't you made enough trouble today?" I said.

Ryan looked at me like he couldn't believe I'd just said that. "Whatever, Traci," he said. Then he got up and walked away.

I turned to Felicia, but she was just sitting there with her mouth open. "Traci!" she began angrily. "What is going on with you? How could you not stick up for Ryan? He's one of your best friends."

"Felicia, he deserved it. He *was* acting totally immature," I said. "And listen . . ." I was going to tell her about what had happened that morning.

"No one deserves to be spoken to like that," she said. "First you pretend your mom is not your mom, and now you let Ryan get walked all over by that jerk. Your priorities are pretty messed up, Traci."

"But listen, Felicia, you don't know the whole story."

"I know as much as I need to know, which is that you are acting totally stuck-up in order to impress some lame guy from Collindale."

"But listen—"

"I don't have time to listen. I'm going to find Ryan and make sure he's okay." And she got up and walked off.

I sat there and tried to finish my lunch, but it was

impossible to eat because I was so upset. I thought about going to find Felicia and Ryan, but I figured I would let them cool down a little. Besides, I was still pretty sure I was right. Adam was being mean, but Ryan had taken it too far. Food fights were totally immature. And embarrassing.

Felicia didn't know what Ryan had done earlier. All things considered, I thought I had a right to be pretty mad at Ryan. No matter how snotty Adam might be, he *had* helped me a lot that morning and maybe even saved our chances at the competition.

I quit trying to eat and decided to go to the business center to check my e-mail.

I had to walk through the lobby to get there, and a big crowd of kids from Wonder Lake were hanging out.

"Hey, Traci! We're going swimming. You want to come?" my friend Deb said.

"No thanks. I think I'll just go and check my e-mail."

"Are you sure? There's a hot tub and a sauna. And there's a high diving board on the pool."

"Yeah, I think I'll just hang back. I can't wait to go to the Sears Tower," I said.

"What time are we meeting?" Deb asked.

"I think two-thirty," I said. And then I laughed and said the line my mother always says: "And don't be late, because you keep fifty people waiting."

One of the reasons that line was so funny was because my mother was almost always late. Ouch. I felt a sharp pang when I remembered my mother and what I had done earlier in the day.

I thought about trying to go and find her right then, but I was worn out. I decided I would talk to her on the Sears Tower trip.

There was a line at the business center. Was everything going to be difficult today?

Finally, my turn came up at the computer.

Message 1

Hi Trace,

Went with Amanda last night to the pizza place and just "happened" to run into your brother. I think he overheard us saying we would be there when he came to say hi to Amanda at lunch. Anyway, we had a good time with him. He can be pretty funny sometimes. Do you think there's any way he might introduce me to that friend of his, Dan Harris? You know, the guy on the football team?

Anyway, I hope you are having a great time. I just know you guys are going to win. We'll miss you at Healing Paws today!

Love,

Arielle

Message 2

Traci,

I'm on my way out the door for Healing Paws

but wanted to tell you hi and that we saw Dave
last night at the Pizza Parlor. It was fun to
hang out with him, and he admitted that he
actually missed you a little!

   Don't worry, I won't forget to tell your
friend Jenny at the hospital that you'll see
her next week and make sure she gets to play
with Peanut. I love that kitten so much, too.

   Don't practice too hard!

                         Love,
                         Amanda

                    Message 3
Hi Trace Face,
   Just a note to say I miss you and good luck
tomorrow.

                         Love,
                         Dad
P.S. This e-mail stuff is pretty cool!

   Well, I thought, *at least my friends and family at
home aren't mad at me.* I was happy to get some
friendly words from Wonder Lake, and I sat formu-
lating my replies for a while.

                    Reply 1
Dear Dad,
   I miss you, too. We've been practicing

                         90

like crazy, and I finally learned that hard
piece perfectly, so I know we are going to
come home with the trophy.

   I hope you and Dave are keeping the house
spotless!

Love,

T

I wanted to tell someone about the situation with
Ryan and Felicia, but I hesitated to tell Arielle. She and
Felicia were usually aligned whenever there were arguments among our group. At first this was really weird
for me because Felicia and I had been best friends from
camp when my family moved to Wonder Lake this
year. I had expected to still be best friends with her, but
instead she seemed much more interested in Arielle.

   It was okay, though, because Amanda had become
a really good friend to me, and we usually agreed
about things when there was a fight.

   I made my decision.

Reply 2

Dear Arielle,

   Hope Healing Paws goes well. Say hi to
everybody for me (human and animal!) and have
a great time. By the way, I know Dave can be
fun sometimes. Mostly when he's asleep (lol).
I'm sure he'll introduce you to Dan, but I

have to warn you that Dan stayed over at our
house last week and he has really stinky feet!

Miss you,

Traci

P.S. We're not coming home without the trophy!

Reply 3

Dear Amanda,

Thanks so much for looking after Jenny at
Healing Paws. Wait until you see her face
when she gets to hold Peanut. Glad you had
fun with my goofy brother last night. I know
he can be fun when he wants to be.

Guess what? I met this kid from Collindale
(a seventh grader) and he taught me a breathing technique that solved all my problems with
the final concert piece! I can play it perfectly now. I spent some time with him working
on it and also hanging out with him, and now
Felicia is all bent out of shape, saying I
don't spend enough time with her. And Ryan
hates Adam, and he's been acting really immature. He interrupted our practice this morning
to make a goofy scene and try to get me to
leave. And then Adam was kind of picking on
Ryan at lunch, so Ryan started shooting peas
at him. I was so embarrassed! And now Ryan AND
Felicia are mad because I didn't stand up for

Ryan. I just think Ryan was acting so goofy, of course Adam blew up and said some mean things.

Anyway, we're all going to the top of the Sears Tower this afternoon, and I can't wait—I've never been up that high in my life.

Hope you have a great time at Healing Paws.

Miss you,

T

It was a little weird that Amanda was hanging out with my brother. It was hard for me to picture him as a guy that girls could like. But I guess from an objective standpoint, he's good-looking enough, and he's athletic and pretty smart. I had known that he liked her for a while. I could tell by the way he would get all interested in what we were doing whenever she was around. And I could also tell because he was always looking for excuses to be around the house when she was over.

What I didn't expect, though, was that she was going to like him back. If they started going out, I sometimes worried, whose friend would she be—more mine than his or more his than mine?

And then what would happen if they broke up? Would Amanda still want to come over to her ex-boyfriend's house?

I took a deep breath. I was worrying over nothing

because I was upset about something else. I was upset because at this moment, all the most important people in Chicago were mad at me.

As I got up to leave, I spotted Felicia on her way *in*to the business center. She got on-line across the room, and I slipped out without saying anything. I decided to let her check her e-mail, and then I'd try to talk to her.

Felicia's e-mail to Arielle

Hey Arielle,
  Chicago is pretty cool. We're staying on the nineteenth floor in the hotel, and you can get dizzy from looking down to the street. Everything is great, except Traci is being a total pain. She has been hanging out with this seventh grader from Collindale, totally blowing off all her friends and even her own mother. This guy is really a jerk. Today he actually threatened to BEAT UP Ryan in the dining room. Anyway, have fun at Healing Paws today. I'll tell you all about our adventures when we get back.
                    See you soon,
                    Felicia

I went to sit in the lobby and wait for Felicia to

come out of the business center. I decided I would try to apologize so we could have a good trip to the Sears Tower together. I didn't want anything to come between me and my friends on a big occasion like that.

I waited for about ten minutes, and she finally came out.

I raised my hand to wave and call her over, but she turned her head away and headed toward the elevator. I ran to catch up, but I got there as the elevator doors were closing.

I couldn't believe she was running away from me.

I punched the up button and waited for another elevator. I would just find her in our room.

I rode the elevator up and looked at myself in the mirrors. There were what looked like millions of me reflected one after another. I looked miserable.

When I got back to the room, she wasn't there. She must have gone to Ryan's room.

There was no way I was going to go up there right now, with both of them that mad at me. Instead I sat down on the bed and cried.

chapter
NINE

A sign in the lobby of the Sears Tower

World's Top 5 Tallest Buildings

Rank	Name	City	Country	Feet	Stories
1	Petronas Towers I and II	Kuala Lumpur	Malaysia	1,483	88
2	Sears Tower	Chicago	USA	1,450	110
3	Jin Mao Tower	Shanghai	China	1,380	88
4	Citic Plaza	Guangzhou	China	1,283	80
5	Shun Hing Square	Shenzhen	China	1,260	69

In 1974, the Sears Tower in Chicago assumed the coveted title of world's tallest building at 1,454 feet. It held this title for twenty-four years until 1998, when the decorative spires atop the Petronas Towers in Malaysia surpassed the Sears Tower by 33 feet. Today the Sears Tower still boasts the tallest occupiable floor and the tallest skyscraper roof in the world.

When the time came to go down to the lobby for the trip to the Sears Tower, I had calmed down a little.

I reminded myself that I had a lot to be glad about. I was perfectly confident in my ability to play the music for the concert. I was lucky enough to be able to compete in this competition in Chicago, one of the greatest cities in the world.

And now I was lucky enough to be getting to go to the very top of one of the tallest buildings in the entire world. The second tallest, actually. I had been excited about this since I first heard we were going to go to Chicago for the semifinals.

In fact, I was the one who pressed my mother to make it one of our sight-seeing stops because I had always wanted to go there.

I love to be up high and be able look down, and to see a long way.

I just knew my friends would have cooled down by now. I really wanted to enjoy this experience with them.

I looked in the mirror before I left the room.

Okay, Trace, you're doing all right, I told myself.

By the time I got downstairs, everyone was boarding the bus already.

"What's with the long face, gal?" the bus driver said to me.

I gave him a smile.

"Oh, a fake smile, that's just what I needed to brighten up my day. Remind me to get you some plastic flowers," he said sarcastically.

Even the friendly bus driver was giving me a hard time?

This really did not seem to be my day.

I got on the bus and looked around. I was almost the last one to board, and I hoped Ryan or Felicia had saved a seat for me.

But the two of them were sitting together, and as I walked by, they turned their heads so they wouldn't have to say hi.

My heart sank.

I walked down the aisle, looking for a seat, but everyone was paired up already. Even my mom was sitting with Midge Worth. I went all the way to the back and took a seat by myself.

I watched out the window as we approached the building. I couldn't help getting excited, even with all the other things that were going on.

It took an amazingly short time to get to the top of the building on the elevator. I thought about how long it would take to walk up all those stairs. I was having a thing for stairs lately.

Then the elevator doors opened.

My heart soared at the view and the feeling of being up so high. The top of this building was one of the highest places you could stand in the world that was human-made.

The spires on top of the Petronas Towers in Malaysia made them officially the highest buildings in the world, but the Sears Tower had a higher observation deck.

I wanted to talk to Felicia and Ryan, but when I looked over at them, they were standing at the wall, looking out, and talking quietly to each other. Every once in a while one of them would glance up and look at me. It was obvious they were talking about me, and I hated to think about what they were saying.

Here I was at the top of the world's second-tallest building, and instead of being excited, I just felt like crying.

Finally, I decided I would just go over to them and try to talk.

I walked up and stood near them. "Can you believe this view, you guys?" I said.

"Yeah," Ryan muttered.

"What I really can't believe is that you're walking up to us and starting a conversation like nothing's wrong," Felicia said angrily.

I sighed. It looked like this wasn't going to be easy. "Well, I know you guys are mad at me, but I don't think you really should be this mad. I mean, after all, here we all are on top of the tallest building in America. Maybe we should be a little nicer to each other," I said.

I knew Felicia wanted me to apologize, but she was making me a little mad. After all, I had approached her. That should count for something in the way of an apology.

"You haven't said you're sorry, Traci. And this time I think you have a lot to apologize for," she said.

I looked at Ryan. He looked like he felt worse than I did. It really wasn't his style to stop speaking to anyone.

"Ryan, are you as mad at me as Felicia is?"

"I guess so. I mean, I don't know, Traci. I *am* pretty mad that you would let that guy be so rude to me." Ryan seemed embarrassed.

"Traci, Ryan doesn't want to say so, but of course he's mad. And if you don't want to say you're sorry, then you should just go stand somewhere else!"

"Fine," I said. "I will." And I walked off.

I tried to admire the view some more. I put a quarter into one of those big telescope machines, but my eyes kept filling with tears, and I couldn't see anything.

I didn't have anyone at all to talk to. I decided that it would be a good time to apologize to my mother. She was standing with Mr. and Mrs. Worth, the chaperons, admiring the view.

"Mom, could I talk to you for a second?"

"Okay, Traci. Let's sit over on that bench." I can tell when my mother is mad just by the look on her face, and right now I could see that she was pretty upset with me.

I began, "Mom, I just wanted to tell you I'm sorry for calling you Ms. McClintic on the elevator. It was just a stupid mistake."

She still looked mad. "I appreciate your apology, Traci, but I'm just not sure why you would do something like that if you weren't embarrassed by me. And can you imagine how that makes me feel?"

"It's n-not that at all, Mom," I stammered. I was so

surprised that she wasn't just forgiving me. "It's just that I . . . I don't know what it was."

"Right. You don't know what it was. You know, I try to be really sensitive to the fact that it's difficult to have your own mother as a teacher. I try to give you your privacy as much as possible. I try not to embarrass you in front of your friends."

"But you never embarrass me, Mom," I protested.

"I find that hard to believe when you're pretending I'm not your mother," she said coldly.

"I'm really sorry, Mom."

"Okay, *Ms.* McClintic," she said, and then walked away.

I couldn't believe it. I had never seen my mother so unwilling to forgive me. When I thought about it, though, I could imagine how much it must have hurt her feelings to have her own daughter refuse to call her Mom.

I felt terrible.

Finally, I just went over to the wall and stared out into the distance, wishing I could be far, far away. Anywhere but here.

I was the first one on the elevator to get down off that building. I never wanted to see the Sears Tower again. I got on the bus, took a seat in the middle, and just waited for someone to sit with me. A nice French horn player named Mary—a seventh grader—sat with me. Poor Mary didn't have many friends, either. And I was glad to share a seat with her.

"What a view, huh?" Mary asked me.

"I know, it was so pretty," I said.

"So how come you're not sitting with your friends?" she asked. Mary is pretty blunt about the questions she asks. I think she kind of scares people away, and that's why she has trouble making friends.

"I had a fight with my friends," I told her.

"Well, you should just apologize and make up with them," she said.

"But you don't even know what the fight was about. What if I wasn't wrong? I shouldn't say I'm sorry if I'm not wrong."

She shook her head. "If your friends are mad at you, you probably did something wrong. It's not worth it to lose your friends because you can't apologize. It's better to just smooth things out and not let little problems become big ones," she said. "Take it from me."

That reminded me of the promise I had made to myself about keeping the peace with my friends. I had decided that I wouldn't let small stuff escalate into big fights and that I would try to get along with my friends no matter what. No disagreement was worth tearing a friendship apart.

It was time I took a look at the way I had been acting and tried to do something to get my friends and my mother to forgive me.

No matter what happened, I had to find a way to make it right. I just didn't quite know how yet.

"You know, I think you're right, Mary. Thanks for the advice."

"Don't mention it," Mary said, and went back to chewing on the end of her hair.

chapter
TEN

Traci's e-mail in box:

```
         YOU HAVE 3 NEW MESSAGES
1. Lose weight while you sleep! Drop 20 lbs. in
   20 days!
2. Want to work at home? Own your own business
   for $0 down!
3. Sales on airline fares at gothere.com. Buy
   now and save!
```

I got off the bus with the intention of going straight to Felicia and talking to her. But she and Ryan had sat in the front, and by the time I got off, they had disappeared.

I went to the computer room after we got back to the hotel. I thought some e-mail from my other friends might help me feel better and give me the strength I needed to fix the situation with Felicia and Ryan and my mother. But when I went into my in box, nothing was there but spam. *What a nobody I am,* I thought.

I sent one e-mail to Amanda so I could feel like I was talking to someone.

```
Dear Amanda,
  We just got back from the top of the Sears
Tower. It would have been really cool, but every-
one is mad at me. Ryan and Felicia won't speak to
me, and somehow I managed to make my own mother
mad at me, too. I'm superbummed, but I've decided
to try and make it right with everybody.
  We are all under a lot of stress from worry-
ing about the competition and from being away
from home, so we have to make sure to be extra
nice to each other.
  I hope things are going okay back home and
that Healing Paws was a great success today.
  Miss you a ton.
                          Love,
                          T
```

After I wrote the e-mail, I reread it and decided it sounded too sad, so I erased it, logged off, and headed up to my room. Felicia wasn't back yet—she was probably hanging out with Ryan—so I just watched TV until it was time to go downstairs for lunch.

I was still feeling really upset when I got on the elevator. Chances were, my apology would do no good. Just like telling my mom I was sorry didn't work, telling Felicia I was sorry probably wouldn't work, either.

The elevator stopped at the sixteenth floor, and the door opened to—Adam.

"Traci!" he said with a big smile. "Going down? I guess I am, too, then."

"Hi, Adam." It was nice that someone was happy to see me, but it only cheered me up a little. After all, Adam was really the source of all my problems in the first place.

"Traci, you look like something's wrong. Are you okay?"

"Yeah, I'm okay. It's just that I had a fight with my friends, and I'm feeling kind of down," I said.

"Well, what happened? You can tell me."

I wasn't sure I should tell him. After all, the fight was mostly about him and what a jerk he was. But it was nice to have someone to talk to. I decided to tell him in a broad way.

"Well, Felicia and Ryan, who you met, are bummed at me because they say I'm not spending enough time with them, and they said I was stuck-up for not defending Ryan at lunch today."

"Obviously your friends are a bunch of immature losers, Traci," he said. "You're better off without them. You can just hang out with me."

This was not the advice I was looking for. There was no way I was better off without them, because I actually really loved them. And I didn't like Adam calling them losers.

But I didn't say anything. I was relieved to at least have Adam to talk to.

We got our dinner, and he kept talking and talking about himself as we got our food from the buffet. The Adam who'd asked me so many thoughtful questions about me and my life seemed to have disappeared.

He was telling me about what a great soccer player he was. "So then I faked out the center and ran past him and took a shot from right across the centerline. Their defense was so lame, the ball went in. So that's how we won the championship."

"I play soccer, too, actually. I'm center on the varsity team."

"It was such a great story that the paper did an article about it with a picture of me. The headline said, 'Defenseman Scores Championship Goal.'"

"That's great, Adam," I said. It was amazing how much he was talking about himself. He didn't let me get in one word.

We went over to the Collindale table to sit down, and I went to take a seat, but Adam pushed me aside with his hip. "Sit here," he told me.

"But I'd rather sit in that seat," I said.

"No, no, I'm sitting here." And he sat down in the seat I wanted. I sat down where he told me to, which was the seat at the very end of the table, where I wouldn't be able to talk to anybody but him.

Adam's friend Jeff was talking about another orchestra he had heard practicing earlier.

"They were so bad, you would not believe it. They sounded like an elementary school orchestra. And they were playing stuff *we* were playing in elementary school."

Everyone at the table laughed at this, and that really spurred him on. "And you should have seen the orchestra director! She weighs like two hundred and fifty pounds, and she had on tight jeans. It was so gross!"

Now all the Collindale kids were in stitches, laughing their heads off. I didn't think it was funny at all to be making fun of other teams. It went against everything I'd ever been taught about sportsmanship.

I was also worried that this kid would start talking about Wonder Lake next.

Someone else started in. "Did you see the kids from Glen Cove? Their orchestra has a private bus, and all their instrument cases match. They think they're so cool. But I have a friend who's heard them play, and he says they stink."

"Yeah, like having color-coordinated instruments and music folders is going to help them play better." A girl at the end of the table snorted.

Adam turned to me. "Did you see them, Traci? What do you think?"

"No, I didn't see them or hear the other orchestra, but if I had, I would *not* be making fun of them," I said. I didn't care if they thought I was a nerd.

Adam laughed. "You're right, Traci. We're so bad. We should be nicer."

Across the room I could see Felicia and Ryan coming into the dining room and going to get their food. Ryan glanced at me and quickly looked away.

Just then there was a bunch of whispering at our table. I could see all the kids whispering behind their hands and pointing. I looked to see who they were looking at, and I could make out what they were saying. "There she is, over there. . . . Oh my God . . . look what she's wearing. When's the last time she washed her hair, do you think?"

I looked over and saw a terribly shy-looking girl about my age walking by with her head down. She was awkward, and she had on old clothes. I remembered seeing her with the rest of the Collindale group earlier.

She had to walk by our table to sit down, and she was trying to give it as wide a berth as possible because it looked like she knew she was being made fun of.

"DOG FACE!" somebody at our table shouted, and then everyone laughed.

"WOOF WOOF WOOF!" another person barked with his mouth behind his hand so no one could officially tell it was him.

The girl made it to her table and sat down by herself with her back to us. I was about to get up and go sit with her, but her friends came in right behind her. There were whispers about them, too, but no shouting. Then they sat down next to her.

I sat there miserably. I could not believe I was sitting with these horrible people. I looked across the room and saw Felicia's laughing face. Then I looked and saw what she was laughing at. Ryan was doing his special Ryan trick of shooting milk through his nose. Totally gross, but also totally funny. I cracked up just looking at him.

"What's funny, Traci?" Adam asked, turning to me. But the sight of his face just made me really mad.

"I was laughing at my friends over there," I told him.

He made a face like he'd just bitten a lemon.

Suddenly, I'd had enough. I'd reached the end of the line with Adam.

I got up from the table.

"Where are you going?" Adam asked.

"See you later," was all I said, and I walked over to Felicia and Ryan.

They looked up, surprised, as I approached the table.

"You guys," I said. "I've been a total jerk. I'm so sorry. I hope you can forgive me."

They were silent for a minute . . . then they looked

at each other. Then Ryan said, "Of course we forgive you, you goofball."

Whew! I was so relieved. I pulled up a chair and sat between them, my good friends, and we talked all about our day.

"Could you believe the view from the Sears Tower? I felt like I could see all the way to the ocean," I said.

"No, Traci, that was the lake," Ryan said. I knew he was joking because everyone knew that had been the lake.

I laughed doubly hard because it was the first time I had laughed all day.

Then I decided to let Ryan have his moment about the juggling attempt in the Collindale practice room. It *had* been sort of funny, just the thing to throw off a stuck-up stuffed shirt like Adam. He *had* given me a lot of help with the clarinet—but even I had to admit that he'd turned out to be a big jerk.

"So what's the king of Collindale up to?" Ryan asked, making a face and then smiling.

I shrugged. "He and his friends are busy saying mean things about people who don't deserve it. I decided I would much rather sit over here."

Felicia nodded. "I'm sure glad you did. I couldn't take much more of Adam."

I sighed. "Well, he really did help me with that breathing thing, but he's not a very nice guy. The whole seventh grade just made fun of this shy girl from their orchestra. It looked like she was going to cry."

"Poor thing," Felicia said.

"I think we got a glimpse of what he's like at lunch today." Then Ryan did a perfectly dead-on imitation of Adam. "Traci, I'll talk to you later, when you're not hanging around with *kindergartners*."

We all went crazy with laughter because his imitation was so good. I think it seemed extra funny because we were all so upset about it before.

Suddenly, Felicia's smile froze on her face. She was looking behind me and Ryan. I turned around to see Adam standing there, looking furious.

He had walked up and heard the last part of what we were saying. He had heard Ryan making fun of him. Ryan saw him, too, and said, "Uhhh, hey." Which made Felicia start to giggle.

"Nice, Traci," he said, his face angry and his voice dripping with sarcasm. "Glad you could find the time to hang out with your kindergarten friends. Their humor is so sophisticated. I can understand why you would want to hang out with them instead of me."

Everyone stopped what they were doing and looked at me.

chapter
ELEVEN

*Writing on the back of Felicia's band notebook
inside two interlocking hearts:*

Felicia and Traci.
Best friends forever.

The whole table was waiting to see how I would react to Adam. Would I just let him insult my friends like I did earlier that day? Or would I stand up for them and tell him to shove off?

There was no question. There was no way I was going to let Ryan and Felicia down like I had before. I'd had enough.

"You're right, Adam," I said, looking him in the eye, "my friends are more mature than you. But the main reason I want to hang out with them instead of you is that you are the rudest, most obnoxious person I have ever met."

Adam looked stunned. I got the idea that no one ever stood up to him in his own world. He searched for the meanest thing he could think of to say.

"Yeah? I might be immature, but I predict that you are going to lose that competition for your school. Your orchestra is lame in the first place, but they don't stand a chance with you squeaking your way through the final piece, Traci! You actually *are* lame at the clarinet. I was lying when I told you that you were good! See you when we collect our trophy, Wonder losers!"

Then he stormed out of the dining room.

The three of us looked at one another, smiling, and then Ryan started laughing. I think we all wanted Adam to hear us laughing as he retreated, so we all laughed long and hard.

Once he was gone and we'd all calmed down a little, Ryan turned to me and said, "Wow! You were good."

"Thanks, Ryan." I grinned. "I was inspired. Nobody talks to my friends like that."

"All right. Now all we have to do is win this competition and prove him wrong," he said.

"Go, Wonder Lake!" Felicia shouted.

"Go, Wonder Lake!" we all yelled.

"Hey, let's go do something," Ryan said.

"Hang on one second, you guys. I just have one more person to apologize to."

I went over to my mom's table, and she saw me coming and smiled. I was relieved to see that the angry look had left her face.

"Traci, hi. I was going to come and find you," she said.

"Hi, Mom. I just wanted to try to tell you again that I'm sorry."

"Sit down, honey," she said, and pulled out the chair next to her. "I'm sorry, too. I shouldn't have gotten so upset."

"Well, I understand why it hurt your feelings."

"You know what? I'm nervous about the competition, too, and that's why I reacted so strongly."

"Oh, Mom, I know you are, and that's why I'm so nervous, too. I've been so afraid that I'll make a mistake and ruin it for everybody. But the worst thing would be to ruin it for you."

"Don't let me hear you talking like that, Traci. You are going to play that piece perfectly. I already heard you do it three times today."

"I hope so, Mom."

"And besides, you know all that stuff I always say? Even though I'm nervous, it's still true: Making beautiful music is the most important thing, not winning a trophy."

"I know, Mom, but—"

"No buts," she said. "As long as everybody on the orchestra plays his or her very best, I don't care if we win a trophy or they boo us off the stage! We'll have won in my mind."

"Okay, Mom. You're the best."

She reached over and hugged me.

"Do you want me to come up for a practice later?" I asked.

"No, honey, I don't. You should go and hang out with your friends and have some fun."

"Are you sure?"

"Of course I'm sure. Now, go on. You've practiced enough for this lifetime."

Felicia, Ryan, and I went up to our room.

"Wow, what a day, you guys," I said. I was so happy and relieved to be hanging out with my good friends again. "You know, I'm really lucky to have friends like you."

"We're pretty lucky, too, Trace," Ryan said. "I had no idea you were such a firecracker. You really gave that jerk Adam a run for his money."

"It was easy because he really deserved it," I said, and the two of them nodded.

"Did you see the look on his face when he realized Traci wasn't on his side anymore? It was priceless," Felicia said.

"Totally. And his lame response that Traci was no good at clarinet when he just helped you learn to play the piece perfectly!" Ryan said, laughing.

But this killed my mood a little. Hearing Adam say that he thought I was a lousy clarinet player and that I would ruin the competition had had a big effect on me. I thought I had mastered that piece in the morning, but now I wasn't so sure.

He was mad when he said it, but it got me thinking. *Maybe he only said I was a good clarinet player because he liked me. Maybe he was putting me on, and I really* am *lame.*

I didn't want to let on that I was worried, though. I had already put my friends through enough trouble that day. They didn't need to go back to reassuring me when they had spent so much time at it earlier.

So I said, "Hey! Let's show Ryan our routine." And I jumped up on the bed to bounce.

"Yeah!" Felicia shouted, joining me.

We turned up the TV loud, and Felicia started by doing a flip from one bed to the other. Then I did the same. Then we did it both at the same time and added the dance moves we had worked up. We kept falling in between the two beds and hitting the wall and generally making a total mess.

We were all laughing hysterically, and pretty soon Ryan jumped up and joined us. He was terrible at flips, though, and he got completely stuck between the wall and the bed.

Just like the day before, we didn't realize anybody was at the door until we heard a loud pounding.

I jumped up and ran to the door and opened it up to the angry face of one of our chaperons, Mrs. Worth.

"I have been knocking and knocking. What in the world are you kids doing in here? Do you have any idea how loud you are?"

"Sorry, Mrs. Worth," I said, trying to look ashamed.

"Look at what a mess this place is. Please turn that

television down right now. I could hear it all the way down the hall!"

Ryan got up to turn it off, and Mrs. Worth spotted him.

"Ryan Bradley! You need to get back to the boys' floor right now! You shouldn't be in here in the first place."

Ryan hightailed it, and we all said we were sorry a few more times. She was still muttering about what a mess we had made as we shut the door.

With the TV off and Ryan gone, the room seemed pretty quiet. We just sat there silently for a little while.

"I wonder how Healing Paws went today," I said.

"I'm sure it was fine," Felicia said, looking at her hands.

"Well, it's a lot of work for your dad with us gone. That's only Amanda and Arielle helping him. And Arielle doesn't do that much in the first place," I said.

"Well," Felicia said, "I think Penny was around to help, too."

"Oh, she was still around today? I'm sorry, Felicia. I know that must be weird for you. Did you talk to your dad on the phone?"

"Yeah. He and Penny left me a message wishing us luck, and I called back and talked to him this morning. He said the two of them were getting the animals ready and waiting for Arielle and Amanda."

"I wish I had been there for you this morning, Felicia."

"Well, you're here now, and I appreciate it," she said, finally looking up.

We got ready for bed and lay down to go to sleep. Felicia fell asleep quickly, and I could hear her deep breathing.

I, on the other hand, started worrying as soon as we shut off the lights. I couldn't sleep at all.

After all that had happened that day, the whole reason we were in Chicago in the first place was to win the competition. In the dark of night, I really had no confidence at all that I could play that piece properly tomorrow.

Sure, I had played it perfectly that morning, but that might have been just a fluke. The more I thought about it, the more I was *sure* it was just a fluke. And the worst thing about these thoughts was that I knew that the more I thought about it, the worse it would get because it was making me more nervous.

I considered getting up and putting my clarinet together and trying to play the piece, but obviously that would wake up Felicia. I would have to wait until morning.

chapter
TWELVE

E-mail response from Amanda to Traci

Trace,

   I think you should just forgive Felicia for
getting mad at you. Spend some more time with
her and it will be fine. You guys should be
concentrating on the competition, not fighting over little stuff. Good luck tomorrow!

Love,

A

E-mail response from Arielle to Felicia

FF,

   If Traci has a chance to hang out with a
seventh-grade guy, maybe you should give her some
space. If he's cute, leave her alone. (If not,
get her out of there.) Say hi to Ryan and Traci.

Love,

Me

"Traci, why don't we call Ryan and have him come down, and we'll all practice for a half hour before breakfast?" Felicia was saying.

I had been up most of the night worrying, and Felicia insisted I tell her what was wrong when we woke up because I was pacing around the room like a madwoman.

"I'm just really nervous," I told her.

"But you played the Mozart piece perfectly yesterday. Just take out your instrument right now and play it for me again, and you'll see that you still know how."

I shook my head. "I'm too afraid. I'm sorry, Felicia, it's just that when Adam said that I stunk last night, it really just stuck with me."

She thought for a second. "Well, we have to do something. I'm calling Ryan."

She dialed and talked to him for a minute while I went into the bathroom to fix my hair. It looked weird because I'd gone to sleep on it wrong, and it had a big cowlick on the side that wouldn't lie flat. Finally, I just put it up into a ponytail.

"He's on his way down," said Felicia when I came out. "We'll just play the music together and you'll see that you have nothing to worry about."

Okay, maybe she's right, I tried to tell myself. . . .

SQUEEEEEAK! The noise came out of my clarinet right at the very beginning of the hardest part of the final piece. I was mortified.

"That's okay," Felicia said. "You're allowed. Just do your new breathing technique and you'll get this, no problem."

SQUEEEEEAK! I felt like crying. I was using the new technique. But I guess I was so, *so* nervous that it just wasn't working.

"Don't worry, Traci, you just need a chance to get warmed up," Ryan said reassuringly. "I just hope I'm not deaf by the time you do get it."

We all stopped and had a good laugh over this. We needed to laugh, to break the tension. After all, these mistakes I was making could cost us the competition in just a few short hours.

I tried again and again. I worked so hard to get my breathing matched to the tempo of the music and to just breathe through my nervousness, but nothing was working.

Every time I played the piece, I messed it up. I was almost crying.

"Okay, I have an idea," Felicia said. "Just hear me out. It might sound a little weird."

"I'll try anything," I said miserably.

"Well, Penny once taught me something called 'creative visualization.'"

"Okay," I said. "What's that?"

Felicia paused, trying to think of the best way to explain it. "The way it works is, you picture yourself, in your mind, getting the thing you want or doing the thing you want. She taught it to me when I was really nervous about that English test we had last week. She said to picture myself getting an A on the test."

"And what did you get on the test?" Ryan asked, leaning forward.

"An A," Felicia said.

"Hmmm . . . So I would what? Picture myself playing the piece perfectly?" I asked.

"Yes, exactly," she said. "You lie down for a few minutes, and we'll be really quiet, and you picture yourself exactly how you would play it and imagine that it sounds perfect."

"Okay, it seems like it's worth a try. I'll do it."

Felicia went and turned off the lights and drew the curtains to make it dark in the room so I could concentrate. I lay down on the bed.

"I think I'll try it, too," Ryan said, lying down on the floor.

"But Ryan, you already play everything perfectly. What do you need to visualize?" I asked him impatiently.

"No," he told me, shaking his head in a way that let me know a joke was coming. "I'm going to visualize *you* playing the piece perfectly, too. Looks like you need all the help you can get."

We both laughed, but Felicia shushed us. She was trying to set the mood.

"Okay. We're ready," she said softly. "Ryan, you have to be perfectly quiet."

"Okay," he said in a serious tone that was rare for him. "Let's begin. Traci, I want you to picture yourself in a beautiful place. Your favorite place. Maybe it's the beach or a field of flowers. Put yourself there and relax. . . . Take deep breaths."

I imagined that I was in a quiet pine forest, walking through the trees. I could feel myself start to relax.

Felicia continued. "Now imagine you're there playing the clarinet. You're playing the piece perfectly. You're the best clarinet player in the entire world."

I pictured my fingers on the keys and the sound of the music when it was played well.

"Keep taking deep breaths," Felicia said quietly. "You're full of confidence and you know what a great clarinet player you are. Picture playing the piece one more time."

I pictured playing it again, perfectly.

"Okay, now lie there for a little while and wake up slowly."

I woke myself up carefully, afraid to knock the relaxation out of me.

"Now play the piece in the same frame of mind," Felicia said, opening up the drapes.

I picked up my clarinet, which had been lying beside me on the bed, and I began to play.

I did it! I played it perfectly.

Felicia and Ryan cheered. "Hooray! I knew you could do it," Felicia said. "Do it again!"

I did. I played it again with no trouble. And one more time just to make sure I wasn't dreaming. Then we all played it together.

It sounded great! We started laughing and cheering. "Go, Wonder Lake!"

"I think we're ready," said Ryan.

We were running early, so we stopped by the business center to check our e-mail before we went in to breakfast. I was hoping to get an encouraging one from Amanda. She's always really supportive, and I had missed talking to her in the last couple of days.

There was no line of people waiting, so Felicia and I went right in. We sat down next to each other side by side at our computers and logged on to check our e-mail.

"Listen to this, Felicia. Amanda wrote me yesterday that I should just be nicer to you and everything would be fine. Guess I should have read my e-mail sooner, huh? She had a good idea—it just took me a little while to figure it out."

"That's funny," Felicia said with a smile. "Arielle says I should just give you some space and let you hang out with this guy Adam—but only if he's cute."

We both laughed.

"Did you get the e-mail from Amanda about Healing Paws?"

"Yeah, she cc'd me. I'm just reading it now."

Dear Felicia and Traci,

Healing Paws was so much fun today, but we really missed you. I was thinking it was going to be really hard work getting all the animals into their cages with only three of us, but Penny showed up to help, and, Traci, so did your brother. Since he's so allergic to animals, he stuck to jobs like hosing down the cages. Anyway, the kids were really cute this week, and they loved the new batch of kittens. Traci, your friend Jenny is doing much better. I told her you say hello, and she says hi back. Her mother told me she is going to go home soon. She played with Peanut the whole time we were there. And she cried a little when she had to say good-bye. But guess what? Jenny's mother secretly talked to Mr. Fiol about adopting Peanut. She is going to bring him home as a surprise for Jenny when she gets out of the hospital! The other big thing that happened is that the little puppy with the black spots got loose on the kids' floor, and Nurse Finkel had to chase him all around to finally catch him. You should have heard the kids laugh at this. It was the funniest thing you ever saw.

Are you feeling ready for the competition?

I just know you are going to win. Break a leg, and write back when you can. Say hi to Ryan.

Love,
Amanda

I also had one from my dad.

Dear Traci,
We're holding up here but cannot wait for the women to get back and wash the dishes (ha-ha). I haven't been seeing much of your brother. I think he's spending some time with your friend Amanda. She's a sweet girl, and if those two get married, you would make the perfect maid of honor. Anyway, I am thinking of you this morning and wishing you the best of luck in the competition. Win or lose, you are the champion of my heart.

Love,
Dad

I had to laugh at my dad's e-mail. It still felt kind of weird for one of my friends to like my *brother*, but deep down I knew they were both great people and would probably be great together. As for me being their maid of honor . . . Well, I chose to put that out of my mind.

Felicia and I signed off and headed for the lobby, where we met up with Ryan again.

I was feeling great and totally confident as we walked in to breakfast. We walked by Adam's table, and he looked up as I passed. I gave him my biggest, brightest smile, just to show him I didn't need him.

"Smile now, Traci, because you'll be crying after we win the competition."

"No, I won't, Adam," I replied. "I'll still be smiling, because no matter who wins, after the competition I'll never have to see you again!"

We just kept walking, and I heard some of the kids at Adam's table laughing at what I'd said, which I'm sure made him plenty mad.

I looked over at Ryan, who was laughing so hard, tears were coming out of his eyes. "*Ouch!*" he said.

As I walked into the ballroom for our final practice, my heart started beating hard. I could feel my teammates looking at me. I had messed up so badly in Friday's practice that I was sure they were all pretty worried about today.

But a lot's happened since Friday, I told myself. *I learned two great techniques for controlling my nervousness, and I'm going to use them to play perfectly today!*

"How are you feeling, Trace?" Wendy, the clarinet one seat ahead of me, came over and sat beside me as I put my clarinet together and adjusted it.

"Pretty good, Wendy. I think we're gonna do great."

"Well, I was surprised not to see you at section

practice yesterday, but tell me more about this new breathing technique. I hear you sounded great!"

"Yeah, it's this amazing way of controlling your breath along with the tempo of the music," I said.

"That sounds so cool," Wendy said. "Do you think you could teach it to me?"

"You bet I could," I told her. I was really glad she didn't seem to be mad about the practice or worried too much about my performance.

We went and sat down together, and I started explaining it to her. Telling Wendy about the technique was good for me because I was practicing it as I was teaching her.

Pretty soon my mother arrived and tapped on the music stand. We all looked up, suddenly quiet.

"Hello, everyone! Today is our big day. Let's have an excellent practice, and let's have an excellent performance."

We played through all the stuff that was easy, and I concentrated on working on my breathing. I also kept picturing myself in the pine forest, playing perfectly, the best clarinet player on earth.

I looked over at Felicia, and she winked at me. The last piece was approaching quickly, and I was struggling to stay calm.

Then I looked over at Ryan. He had his violin up to his chin, and he smiled a big grin at me and crossed his eyes.

I thought about the fact that I had really become good friends with him on this trip. He was such a great guy in so many ways. The more I got to know him, the more I liked him.

And it was while I was thinking about this, and how lucky I was to have such supportive friends, that I played through the last piece with no problem at all. It flowed along like water, and as we finished, my mother put down her baton and clapped furiously.

"Terrific!" she yelled. "Fantastic! What fabulous musicians you all are. Thank you so much for all your hard work. I don't care if we win or not—I am so proud of you all, I could burst," she said happily. "But we are going to win, by the way!"

"Go, Wonder Lake!" Ryan shouted.

"GO, WONDER LAKE!!!" the whole orchestra responded.

"Hooray, Ms. McClintic!" Ryan yelled.

"HOORAY, MS. MCCLINTIC!!!" the rest of the kids responded.

"Hooray, Mom!" I yelled.

She looked at me and smiled.

As we packed up to leave, Felicia turned to me. "You realize that the next time we play this music, it will be for the performance?"

"I know. It seems like we were waiting and waiting for this day forever, and now it's finally here," I said.

"Traci, I know you're going to be fantastic in this performance," Felicia told me.

"Well, I hope so. But how do you know?"

"Because you worked so hard for it. You've been practicing nonstop, and it'll pay off when it comes time to perform. I just know it."

"Thanks, Felicia. I think you may be right," I said.

"Of course I'm right. Now let's go and do our nails for the performance. We have to make sure we look good so that when we win, we can win in style."

"Now you're talking. Looking good is the most important thing, right?" I laughed, going back to our old joke.

We said good-bye to Ryan and took the elevator up to our room to have some serious girl time and prepare for the competition.

chapter
THIRTEEN

From the Wonder Lake Middle School Orchestra
Handbook

<u>Required Dress for Performances</u>

<u>Girls</u>

    White blouse

    Black shoes

    Natural-colored hose or no hose

    Long black (at least midcalf- to ankle-length) skirt (must
be approved by Ms. McClintic)

    No dangle or drop earrings or necklaces

<u>Boys</u>

    White-collared shirt

    Black shoes (no tennis shoes!)

    Black socks

    Black dress pants (no cargo pants)

    Long dark tie (please, no bow ties)

"Should I tuck this in or leave it out?" Felicia asked as
she was getting dressed.

Felicia looked really great in her concert clothes. She had on a tight black skirt and these amazing black high heels. She had borrowed from Arielle a white blouse that was tailored at the waist.

"I think my mom is going to say that we all have to have our shirts tucked in," I said.

"I know, but this shirt was really made to be left out. I think it looks better out." She adjusted it in front of the mirror, trying it both ways.

"Just ask my mom when we go down," I said as I pulled on my skirt.

I felt a little frumpy in my plain knee-length black skirt and lace-up black dress shoes, but Felicia had put my hair in a braid on top of my head, and that looked really good.

Also, my mother had said we could wear makeup, and after we got dressed, we put on a little bit of blush and lip gloss.

"Try this one," Felicia said, handing me a different shade of blush.

I was focused intently on getting ready because I was feeling nervous. And worrying about whether to wear stockings or not took my mind off worrying about the competition.

Felicia helped me some more with my makeup, and then I did hers.

When we were finally ready, we stood in front of the mirror together, two friends.

"We look pretty good," she said.

"We do," I agreed. "You know, even if we don't win, we'll be the best-looking musicians," I told her jokingly.

"And that's the most important thing," she joked back.

"Right, it's not whether you win or lose, it's about making beautiful music and looking pretty!" I said.

It was okay for us to joke about this because we both knew that we were only kidding. We both really wanted to win.

We were solemn as we gathered up our music and instruments and headed for the elevator. The other kids from our orchestra were coming out of their rooms, too, and we greeted them quietly. It was a big day, and we were nervous.

Down in the lobby about a million dressed-up kids with instruments were buzzing around, headed in one direction or another.

"Holy cow. Look at that," Felicia said, pointing behind me.

I turned around to see a group of thirty kids in *tuxedos* coming off the elevator. Carrying their instruments, they headed for the concert hall.

"That must be the Glen Cove team. Adam told me they go all out for the competition," I said, staring after them.

We went to our staging area, which was the ballroom where we had practiced.

The plan was that we would get our instruments

and music ready in the staging area and leave them set up there. We would then join the audience and watch the performances until just before our turn, when we would go to the staging area and wait to go onstage.

Everyone was talking excitedly in the ballroom as they put together their music.

Ryan came over, violin in hand, when he saw us coming in.

"Hey, girls. Wow, you look great!"

"Thanks, Ryan. You too," Felicia said.

I couldn't believe how good Ryan looked with a tie on. It made him look much older. I was impressed.

"Are you nervous about your solo?" Felicia asked him.

"Yeah, totally. Can you imagine if I mess it up with the spotlight on me? I don't even want to think about it. I do better if I just pretend I'm not scared out of my mind."

"I've never heard you make a mistake yet," I said.

"Well, wouldn't this just be the perfect moment? There's a first time for everything."

We all laughed.

"How are you feeling, Trace?" he said, looking at me intently. And then all of a sudden what I felt nervous about was talking to him. It was weird because we'd been hanging out constantly on this trip and I hadn't even thought about it, but right then, I was a little tongue-tied and sweaty in his presence.

So much so that I forgot to answer. . . .

"Traci?" he said.

"Earth to Traci." Felicia laughed.

"Oh, sorry, you guys. I'm okay, I guess. A little nervous. But not like before."

"All right, let's hear your solo, Ryan," Felicia said.

He put his violin up to his chin, paused for a minute, and then played the whole thing but sped up so it wouldn't take so long.

"Sounds good," said Felicia.

I didn't say anything at all, and they both looked at me funny.

"Traci, tell me you're all right. You're so quiet."

"Sorry, guys," I said, trying to be more upbeat. "I'm just getting in the zone."

My mom came to the door of the ballroom. She looked beautiful in a long simple black dress and hoop earrings. Everybody always says my mom is really pretty.

"Hey, Wonder Lake musicians! I see you all are getting ready. You should be in the auditorium to take your seats in fifteen minutes. We're the sixth to perform, so after the fourth program—that'll be Glen Cove—please come on back in here, and we'll get prepared to play."

"Round of applause for the best orchestra director in the world!" Ryan said loudly.

Everybody put down their instruments and clapped. My mom smiled and blushed a little.

I felt really proud that she was my mom.

*   *   *

The concert hall was part of the hotel, and it was really big. It seated about a thousand people, and almost all of the seats were filled. It was modern, with clean lines, everything in shades of blue. We went to our reserved seats and looked around. I was sitting between Felicia and Ryan, and when Ryan saw the Glen Cove group in their tuxes, he crossed his eyes.

"Traci, can you ask your mom if *we* can wear tuxes next year? I feel underdressed."

Felicia and I giggled.

"I don't know, Ryan. I think they look pretty good," Felicia said.

We were still laughing when I spotted the Collindale crowd coming in. Their seats were behind ours, so I could avoid looking at them. The last thing I needed right now was to hear Adam tell me I stunk again.

"Don't look behind you, because there's a cock-roach at six o'clock," Felicia whispered.

"Thanks, Felicia. I saw him, and I'm just not going to look," I said.

There were twelve orchestras in the competition, and each was performing a program about fifteen minutes long. The first school was onstage, warming up. The familiar cacophony of instruments being tuned and little snippets of the music to come filled our ears.

As the lights dimmed and the announcer came out onto the stage, I found myself getting nervous. But was

I nervous about performing, or was I nervous about sitting so close to Ryan in the dark?

The truth is, mostly I was thinking about Ryan and how great he looked in that tie. I wasn't thinking about music at all.

I forced myself to focus. I really wanted to hear the other programs. Were we better than the others? Worse?

"These guys are good," Ryan leaned over and whispered to me. But almost as soon as he said it, someone in their percussion section made a huge mistake. A drummer got out of rhythm, and his mistake threw off the rest of the players, and the conductor struggled to bring them back into the music.

"Scratch that. I guess I jinxed them," he said.

"Shhhhhhh!" Felicia reprimanded him.

The programs went on, and I was just as aware of Ryan's presence next to me as I was of the music. Soon enough, it was time for us to get up and go to the ballroom. As the applause began for the fourth orchestra—Glen Cove—we got up and made our way up the aisle.

"Guess wearing tuxes doesn't make you play better, huh?" Ryan joked.

"Hush, Ryan. Don't be mean," Felicia said.

Ryan was right that they weren't that great. So far—and maybe I was a little biased—we seemed like the best among those I had heard.

I started to imagine that we could win, picturing what it would feel like to bring home the trophy.

But then that started to make me think about what it would be like to be the reason we didn't win, and I started to feel sick with nervousness.

I picked up my clarinet and went into the corner of the ballroom to try to calm down a little. I breathed deeply and imagined myself in the forest. It was lovely there. Why couldn't I just stay in the forest, under a tree, until this was all over? I played the Mozart piece to myself, and it sounded fine.

I looked back over at the whole orchestra. My mom was helping an oboe player adjust his instrument. Ryan was tuning his violin again. Felicia was doing what I was doing—standing off to the side, playing her part to herself.

The room was filled with the noises of the instruments and the low talking of all the kids.

Suddenly, my mom looked up and saw me looking over. She smiled and started walking toward me, taking little steps in her high heels. I went to meet her halfway.

"Traci, you are going to be wonderful," she said, and wrapped her arms around me in a big hug. I realized then that it really didn't matter if we won or lost. The weekend had been one of the best and most exciting experiences of my life.

"Thanks, Mom. I'm going to make you proud."

"You already do, honey. Come on. It's time to go and make beautiful music!"

She went to the door of the ballroom. We could hear the applause of the audience in the concert hall.

It was our turn to take the stage.

"Let's go, Wonder Lake!" my mom shouted from the door, waving us through with her whole arm.

Everyone grabbed instruments and music and filed through the door. The air was electric with excitement and nervousness.

"Break a leg, McClintic," Ryan whispered to me as we went to take our seats on the stage.

The stage was bright and hot and the audience was dark, so there was no chance I'd accidentally see Adam. In fact, it was hard to see the audience at all, and that was a good thing.

I pretended I was in the forest with the rest of the orchestra. I breathed. I reminded myself how well I knew the music.

My mother tapped her music stand with her baton. She smiled down at me as we all sat up and readied our instruments.

And we played. We played better than we had ever played before.

Midway through the program, Ryan stood up for his violin solo. The spotlight trained on him, he played it effortlessly, a look of total concentration on his face. I was struck again by how good-looking he was. And how talented. It was kind of strange to hear such beautiful music coming from the class clown, but that's part of what makes Ryan so interesting. I realized I was watching him intently, and I blushed.

I didn't really have time to get nervous, because before I knew it, the final song was starting, and I didn't even think. I just played, and I played every note perfectly. All my hard work paid off.

Just as suddenly as we had started, we were finished.

We got up to bow, and the applause was so loud, it hurt my ears. There was no doubt about it. I knew we had been great.

As we took our seats again after the performance, I was elated.

Ryan rushed to catch up to me in line so he could sit next to me. He was wearing his familiar grin. "I told you that you could do it, Traci. Can you believe how good we were?"

"What about you, Ryan? You were amazing," I said, and actually felt myself blushing a little again.

We watched the Collindale team walk onto the stage. They looked really good—the boys had black blazers to match their pants and ties, and the girls' skirts all matched. And they sounded good, too. It was true that they played music that was very advanced.

"They're pretty good," Felicia whispered to me.

"I know, they really are," I agreed.

As they finished, with a complicated and beautiful finale, I was feeling like there was no way we would beat them. And I actually didn't care. They were excellent musicians, and if they won, it would be because they deserved it.

But we had done our best. We had nothing to be ashamed of.

We sat through the rest of the competition, but none of the other orchestras compared to the Collindale performance.

I was really relieved to be finished with the performance. Now the only nerve-racking thing left to worry about was the awards ceremony.

There was a brief intermission before the awards were to be given out, and we all went and stood in the lobby.

While I got a drink at the water fountain, Ryan leaned over and whispered, "Don't look now, Traci— we have an enemy approaching from the left." I looked over and saw Adam and his friends walking by. He caught my eye.

"Glad you didn't blow it for your whole orchestra, Traci. Guess you have me to thank for that."

And he walked off before I could think of anything to say to him.

"What a *jerk*," said Felicia.

Just then, the announcer called from the stage that the awards ceremony was about to begin.

We all filed back in and took our seats.

The first awards went to the best instrument section in each category. Wonder Lake won best percussion, and all our drummers went up and took their award triumphantly. We all clapped like crazy. We were so proud!

Then came the awards for best solo. I was hoping Ryan would win, and I thought he really deserved it. He was acting like he didn't care, and maybe he didn't. But I knew his mother would certainly be proud. And so would I.

The announcer said, "And the award for best solo violin performance goes to Ryan Bradley, of Wonder Lake Middle School!"

Felicia and I jumped to our feet, clapping and cheering like crazy. Ryan went up and accepted the award, looking bashful. On his way back to his seat, he stopped and gave my mom a hug. I saw her hug him back, hard.

"And now, boys and girls, ladies and gentlemen, the moment has come. I am about to announce the winner for best overall performance of an orchestra, the winner of the Illinois State Semifinal Competition.

"Third place goes to . . . South End Middle School of Westridge!"

The orchestra director went up and accepted the certificate, smiling.

My stomach was feeling jumpy. We hadn't won third place. Did that mean we'd won second place . . . or first?

"Second place goes to . . . Wonder Lake Middle School of Wonder Lake!"

We went wild cheering as my mother went up to claim our certificate. She looked terrific, and she thanked the presenter as she accepted.

She came back to where we were sitting, and we all gave her a standing ovation.

It probably looked to the rest of the audience like we were giving ourselves a standing ovation, but we didn't care. We wanted my mother to know how proud we were.

"If I could ask for some quiet in the audience, please," the announcer said. He was talking to us because we couldn't seem to stop cheering.

"And the winner of the first place overall award, the champion of the Illinois State Semifinal Competition is . . . Collindale Middle School!"

Our whole orchestra made a point of clapping loudly for their win as their director went up to accept the award.

I really wasn't disappointed that we hadn't won first place. We'd played our best. We'd made beautiful music, and what else really matters?

In the lobby after the awards ceremony, there was a reception with hors d'oeuvres and sparkling apple juice for all the competitors.

As we were toasting one another, I heard Felicia say, under her breath, "Oh, brother. Here we go again."

I spun around and there was Adam, flanked by a couple of his friends. He had a snide, I-told-you-so look on his face.

"So how's it feel to *lose*, Traci?" he said.

I just looked at him. A whole bunch of kids from Wonder Lake were watching. I guess word of Adam's nastiness had gotten around.

"Actually, we didn't lose at all, Adam. We played well and we had a great time. Congratulations on your win," I said with a little smile.

He just looked at me, not knowing what to say, his face trying to find an expression.

I had bested him by simply being nice.

All he could manage was a lame, "Whatever . . ." before walking off.

"Ouch!" Ryan said, grinning at me.

chapter
FOURTEEN

**T-shirts Ms. McClintic had made
for the entire orchestra as a surprise**

Front:
I Survived the Wonder Lake Middle
School Orchestra Illinois State
Semifinal Competition!

Back:
Making Beautiful Music Wherever We Go!

I woke up on Monday morning feeling better than I had in weeks. Felicia was still asleep, and I lay in bed, thinking about everything that had happened over the weekend.

When we had arrived in Chicago, I'd been so worried about whether I'd be able to play the Mozart piece that I wasn't thinking about anything else.

But along the way, in learning to play the piece and in actually performing it, I had learned so many other things, too.

I had learned about the value of my friends, for one thing.

And I had learned that people—like Adam—are not always what they seem.

And I had learned that it takes a lot of hard work to be really good at something.

I was really looking forward to the day coming up. We were headed to the Chicago Museum of Contemporary Art for a few hours, and then . . . we were going home.

As much as being away was exciting and interesting, I couldn't wait to get home to my own house and my own room. And even though Wonder Lake was only a few months old for me, it already felt completely like my home.

"Hey, you're up early," Felicia said as she woke up.

I had pulled a chair over to the window and was sitting with my feet up, looking out at the view.

"Yeah. I was just thinking about how fast this weekend went by. It seems like so much stuff happened, but now the trip's almost over," I said.

"I know, it feels like it was really long and really short. I'll be happy to get home," Felicia said.

"I was just thinking that, too," I told her.

"Should we get dressed and go down to breakfast?" she asked.

"Yes, let's."

I decided that I was going to wear the plaid miniskirt today. I knew I looked good in it, and I

147

found myself thinking of wanting to look good in front of Ryan.

"Hey, should we call Ryan and tell him to come and meet us?" I asked Felicia.

"Yeah, if you want. But we'll probably just see him down there."

Just then the phone rang.

I picked it up. It was Ryan, pretending to be Adam. "Hi, is this the room of the Wonder Losers?" he said in his best Adam voice. "Because I've got news for you. You guys are lame!"

I laughed. "Hey, Ryan. Do you want to meet us at breakfast?"

But he had already hung up the phone.

"You know, Trace, do you ever get the idea that Ryan kind of . . . well . . . likes you?" Felicia asked me.

My heart felt like it skipped a beat at this question.

But I didn't have time to answer because there was a knock at the door.

I opened it to see Ryan.

What did Felicia mean by that? Did she think that he liked me? There was no way I could ask her now. I let Ryan into the room. He walked right to the window.

"Wow, you really can't see anything from down here on this lower floor! You poor girls!" Ryan joked.

Actually, it was a very clear day and you could see for about fifty miles.

"Come on, guys," I said, grabbing Ryan's hand and

then Felicia's. "Let's go down to breakfast. It's time to start the day."

I never did get a chance to say good-bye to Adam. Before I knew it, we were lining up at the bus with our instruments.

I handed my clarinet case to the driver, and he gave me a big smile. "My girl's happy again, huh? Well, all right!"

I was already smiling, so I gave him an even bigger smile—a real one this time.

When we were all on the bus, my mother got up in front and gave a little speech.

"Musicians, I am as proud of you as I could be. We played our best! We won second place! We made beautiful music, and nothing is more important than that."

We all applauded her and cheered.

She went on. "I have a surprise I had made for you all right here."

And she lugged a box full of something up the stairs of the bus.

Inside were special semifinalist shirts for everybody. On the front, they said: *I Survived the Wonder Lake Middle School Orchestra Illinois State Semifinal Competition!* And on the back: *Making Beautiful Music Wherever We Go!*

The first person she gave one to was the bus driver. He put his on over his sweater and stood up and spun around, modeling it for us as my mother passed the rest out to the kids.

We all laughed, and then everybody did what he'd done and put the shirts on over our clothes.

Our final stop on the trip was the Chicago Museum of Contemporary Art. Then we were headed home.

We looked a fine sight walking across the shiny marble floors of the museum in our new T-shirts.

We had a couple of hours to explore the place on our own before we had to meet back for the ride home.

"Let's go check out the French Impressionists," Ryan said.

"Okay, sounds good to me," said Felicia. "What are French Impressionists?"

"They were some guys in France who broke all the rules and decided to paint things as they felt about them, instead of as photographs," Ryan explained.

"Wow, that sounds cool," I said. Ryan is so surprising. He knows about so many different things, and he keeps it to himself until suddenly a topic comes up and he can tell you all about something.

Like French Impressionists, for instance, who turned out to be beautiful.

We looked at a painting by Monet, who I had already heard of, and Ryan explained how he painted the light and commented on the way it changed from one part of the day to the next or from one season to the next.

"And this made people really mad at the time," he said.

"But I don't understand why," Felicia said.

"I guess because they thought a painting should just look like exactly what you could see with your eyes when you looked at it. This was a whole new way of painting something, and people thought it wasn't art at all."

"But it's so beautiful," I said.

"I know, isn't it? They just had to open their minds to what was right there in front of them, even if it was scary to them," he said.

I didn't get exactly what he was saying, but it seemed like he was talking about more than just the art.

Was he trying to tell me something? I thought so, but I couldn't tell what.

But having deep and educational conversations about art wasn't all we did.

In a section of the museum that didn't seem to have any guards, he took off his shoes and convinced us to do the same, so we were in our sock feet.

"Ryan, I don't know if this is such a good idea," Felicia said warily.

"Watch me," he yelled as he went running across the floor, then stopped suddenly and slid twenty feet across the slick marble surface.

"Wow!"

Felicia and I followed suit. We took a running start, then slid like ice-skaters across the floor.

"This could be an Olympic event!" I half shouted, half whispered.

"This is the greatest thing I've ever done!"

Felicia and I collided and went sprawling. Just then a guard appeared and then another. They didn't look too happy.

I was afraid they were going to kick us out of the museum, and we'd have to wait outside in the cold for the rest of the group. Or worse, I was afraid they'd arrest us, and my mom would have to come and get us at the police station.

Then I noticed that one of the guards was trying not to smile.

Smiley didn't say anything, but the other one—the mean-faced one—said, "You kids need to put your footwear back on immediately. What you are doing breaks about seventeen different museum rules."

"Sorry, sir," Ryan said.

"Yeah, we're really sorry." I tried to look ashamed.

"Uh-huh. What group are you with? We are going to have to inform your chaperons that you were engaged in some trouble."

Oh no! My mother would be so mad at us. And on the last day of the trip, just as things were starting to look up.

I decided to talk because the other two seemed frozen.

"Um . . . we're with the Wonder Lake Middle School orchestra, sir."

The other one, the smiley one, spoke up.

"Orchestra? Did you say you were with the orchestra?"

"That's right, sir, we're here for the Illinois

State Semifinal Competition." I smiled nervously.

"Well, how about that," he said. "I was there yester-day. My daughter plays flute for one of the other schools. Not that they won a darn thing. What are you? Wonder Lake? You all won second place, didn't you?"

"Yes, sir, we sure did," Ryan said.

"Congratulations. That's like winning first, actually, because nobody ever wins first but those Collindale kids. They dedicate their lives to the orchestra, and they always win."

He shook our hands in congratulations.

"What do you say we let these kids off with just a warning, Fred?"

Officer Grumpy Face didn't look like this was his favorite idea. He looked like he wanted to object because telling our group leader on us would be the most fun he'd had all day. But he grudgingly said, "All right. But no more monkey business, kids."

"Thank you, sir, we'll behave," Ryan said.

"We promise. Thank you so much," I said, quite relieved.

We had our shoes back on by now, and the nice guard congratulated us again. Then the two of them left us there. Mean Face looked back one more time as if he knew we were going to take our shoes right back off and go sliding into some priceless sculpture, but he finally disappeared.

We wandered around some more and found a bench

to sit on that gave us a view of a huge painting that looked like someone had just thrown a bunch of paint on it.

"Will you two wait for me here while I go and find the bathroom?" Felicia said.

"Sure," Ryan said. "I think we need some time to contemplate this painting so we can learn what it means."

"I think it means somebody was walking and they tripped and splashed paint on this canvas and the museum came and picked it up and hung it on the wall," Felicia said as she walked away.

We laughed, and then we sat there in silence for a few minutes. It was the first time I had been alone with Ryan that I could really think of, and we were sitting really close on the small bench.

I started to get a little nervous.

"Ryan, I was really proud of you, winning that solo award. You played great, and I know it made my mother really happy."

"You know, Traci," he said, but his voice squeaked a little. He cleared his throat. "Actually, I wanted to tell you, I was really impressed with the way you handled that guy Adam."

"Thanks, Ryan. But I know it took me a while to get it right," I said. I wasn't that proud of my track record in the Adam department. I had let him be rude to my friends for two days.

"But most people would never have gotten it right. Most people would have been intimidated by him.

But you weren't scared at all," he said. "Anyway, it meant a lot to me."

I wondered what Ryan was saying. Was he telling me that it meant a lot that I'd stood up to Adam for his sake?

Ryan almost never talked in a serious tone of voice like this, and it was making me even more nervous. But nervous in a good way.

"What I mean is," he said, hesitating. "What I mean is . . . that your friendship means a lot to me. I mean, really a lot, and I . . ."

He just let the unfinished sentence hang there. It wasn't like Ryan to be at a loss for words.

I realized that he was trying to tell me something, but maybe he was afraid. He had a very nervous look on his face, and I could tell he meant that he was glad that I hadn't gone for Adam because maybe he had the same feelings for me as I had for him.

My heart leaped at the thought. It looked like we were both too shy to say these things out loud.

"Ryan?" I said. I had a hard time looking at him because I was so nervous.

"Yes, Traci?"

"I think I know what you mean."

He took a breath to say something else, but just then Felicia appeared, and the moment was over.

"I got so lost, you guys. I thought I was never going to find you. But I found some sculptures that we have to go and see. They're so weird, Ryan is going to have to explain them to us."

As we got up and followed her out, I looked at Ryan and caught his eye one more time. He just looked back, not making any jokes, and gave me a small, almost shy smile.

I had such mixed feelings when it came time to get back on the bus to go home. I was sad to leave, but at the same time, I couldn't wait to get home.

The bus driver was sitting at the steering wheel as we got on, and he had a nickname for each of us as we boarded.

Ryan was, "Hey, Mr. Tall Man."

To Felicia he said, "Have a nice trip, brown-eyed lady."

I got on behind Felicia and he said, "Looks like you turned that frown permanently upside down. I didn't think you looked like the mopey type, sweetheart."

He was right. I wasn't the mopey type. And now I had a million and one reasons to be happy.

We were coming back to Wonder Lake with second place in the competition, and I had a secret suspicion that Ryan might like me as much as I liked him.

What a terrific weekend!

A lot of us slept for most of the ride home, including me and Felicia. That is, we slept until Ryan, back to his usual joking self, accidentally woke us up as he tried to cover us in pretzels that he placed one at a time so we would wake up with pretzels all over us.

We stayed awake for the rest of the trip into Wonder Lake, and it was just starting to get dark as we pulled into town.

It was great to see the familiar landmarks, like the pizza parlor and the park. When we pulled up into the school parking lot, we got a huge surprise!

A whole bunch of friends and family had come to the school to welcome us back. They had painted a huge banner that said:

CONGRATULATIONS, WONDER LAKE ORCHESTRA!

I saw Amanda and Arielle holding up the banner.

"Wow, look at this!" Felicia said.

We all rushed off the bus and over to our friends.

I hugged Amanda and then Arielle, and then I felt a tap on my shoulder. I turned around to see my dad.

"Dad!" I gave him a big hug.

"Congratulations, honey. I heard you were terrific."

"You know who was terrific, actually, was Mom," I said.

"I know, I'm trying to find her."

"There she is, getting off the bus." I pointed.

I watched as he went over to her and kissed and hugged her. I was so glad that my mom was happy and that things had worked out so well.

What a great trip.

I went back over to my friends.

"So tell us everything!" Arielle said. "What happened with the seventh grader, Traci? The clarinet player?"

Ryan, Felicia, and I just laughed.

"Let's just say I think Traci made a lasting impression on him!" Ryan said.

We all laughed again.

"I can't wait to hear this story," Amanda said, laughing with us.

"Yeah, we have a lot of catching up to do," Felicia said.

I was truly happy. The only thing better than getting to go on an exciting trip is getting to come home to good friends and family.